THE VAMPIRE OATH

THE VAMPIRE OATH

THE VAMPIRE DEBT: BOOK FOUR

USA TODAY BESTSELLING AUTHOR

ALI WINTERS

www.aliwinters.com
www.thevampiredebt.com

ADULT ROMANTASY

Shadow World: The Vampire Debt

The Vampire Debt

The Vampire Curse

The Vampire Court

The Vampire Oath

The Vampire Crown

Shadow World: Standalones

The Vampire Trap

Wicked Prince of Frost

Stand Alone Titles

High Stakes

YOUNG ADULT

The Hunted Series

The Reapers

The Exodus

The Moirai

The Fallen

Flirting with Death (a short story)

The Hunted series Omnibus

In The End duology

Sound of Silence

Light in Darkness

In The End Omnibus

Stand Alone Titles

Cast In Moonlight

Favor of the Gods

Shadow World
SUNFAL
Nightwich
CASTLE
Progsdale
Durford
Littlemire
Valeburn

MOUNTAINS
Sangate
Gloamfarrow
Windbury
Galeport
Murhelm
Crescent Isle
Stormvale
N

For Trish

CHAPTER ONE

CLARA

The fingers around my throat tighten, pressing in and pinning me against the wall. Cassius brings his face within an inch of mine, snarling. The sharp points of his fangs glint, stark white in the flickering torchlight.

"You are a *slayer*, Clara. Stop acting as if you aren't."

I grab his wrists. My fingers fumble to remove his hand.

It's no use... he's too strong.

Cassius loosens his grip, and I can finally take a shallow breath of air into my lungs. It burns against my aching throat.

"How can I act like a slayer if I have no idea what that means?" I grind out.

His only response is an animalistic growl. I claw at his skin hard enough to make a human bleed. Even as I dig my nails in, his flesh heals the minor cuts instantly. I doubt it lasts long enough for him to even feel it at all.

"The title has power, and you need to claim it."

I stop struggling and indicate his hand keeping me in place. "Clearly, I am not any stronger than before."

Cassius's face drops, unamused with my ignorance. "Not literally," he says flatly. "It is a title that makes vampires fear you."

"Then it's nothing more than a label marking me for the crime of killing a few vampires before they could kill me. It means *nothing* to me," I scoff.

Jerking my leg, I go to knee him in the stomach. He sees it coming and moves in and to the side, too close for me to get any momentum.

"Words have power, little bird."

Arching my back against the wall, I try to push off, but his leg keeps me in place. My efforts amount to nothing more than a dying insect's would to a horse.

"How would they know?"

"There isn't a vampire within this city who doesn't already know who you are. The power of demons runs through our veins—even lesser vampires." He says, dark and low. The fingers around my neck tighten again. "We are immortal, possessing the strength of twenty men... and for a mortal to kill three and live to tell the tale? Now that is something to fear."

Without warning, Cassius releases me and steps back. I stumble sideways and use the wall for support as I gasp and choke.

The ache fades after a moment as my body begins to heal, thanks to the mark. My partially crushed airway reforms as I struggle for ragged breath after ragged breath. Then the rawness inside my throat subsides.

More than three, I want to say, but keep silent. The less anyone knows, the better.

I glare through the curtain of my hair at Cassius. He has found this new ability to be "helpful" in our training sessions, having decided that pain and minor injuries will help me learn faster.

"You're not concentrating. If you don't put your head into it, you will end up dead."

"I am," I say. "You have me training two times a day for hours on end... It's all we do—*I'm tired*."

He crosses his arms over his broad chest and chuckles humorlessly. "You're not tired—you're pouting." Lightning fast, Cassius closes the distance between us in a single stride. His hand wraps around my arm, forcing me to turn and face him. "You can't afford to stay weak."

My nostrils flare as I hold in the spike of anger igniting. "And a title will not make me strong," I grind out through gritted teeth.

There's a flash of his white sleeve as he brings his other arm up. I react on instinct and duck, using my forearm to block the strike. Pain vibrates down to the bone as we connect, but I ignore it and kick out, aiming for the inside of his leg just above the knee.

Cassius leaps out of reach just before I connect. I lunge forward, ready to deliver the series of strikes we've been working on all morning, and suddenly, he's behind me. Twisting at the waist, I turn, knowing a hit will come.

Except, I don't block in time.

His fist connects to my shoulder just hard enough to knock me off balance. The heel of my boot catches on one of the uneven floor stones. Cassius reaches for me as I fall back.

There's a deep thud, an explosion of stars as my head strikes, and then nothing.

"Are you going to let this vampire kill you?" Varin's familiar raspy voice asks. The damned demon has once again dragged my unconscious mind down to their cell.

I groan, pressing a hand to my throbbing head. "What do you want?"

"Don't ask questions you already know the answer to." Dark, skeletal hands splay over the floor in front of me. Varin's taloned fingers dig into the stone as if it's nothing more than dry sand, dragging their upper body forward and into the light that illuminates one side of their face. "Bargain with me and quit allowing that sadistic vampire to pummel you within an inch of your life. I can give you all the power you need."

I laugh. It would be tempting… if making bargains with demons didn't lead to a guaranteed painful death… or worse. Nothing good has ever come from such dealings.

"I could have all the power I need, but you would have complete control over me. At best, I would die quickly doing your bidding."

The demon chuckles. "Perhaps if I were a lesser demon, that would be your fate."

I step back. Their words, filled with humor and spoken so lightly, fill me with dread.

Varin lifts a hand. Each movement slow and graceful as if they are underwater. Turning a palm up, they unfurl their fingers, once more offering the silver ring that would bind us.

I swallow the lump forming in my throat.

"Take it, Clara. Take it and—"

Something cool and smooth slides against my cheek.

"Not now, Asmod," Cassius chides softly.

Fuck, that hurt.

Cold hands pat my cheeks, ripping my consciousness away from Varin and back into the training room. Blinking into the torchlight that seems much brighter than before, I force my gaze to focus on the blurry face before me. Golden light gilds the edges of pale hair.

Cassius's eyes, the same dark green color of Asmod's scales, come into focus. He holds me up at my shoulders and looks at me expectantly. "Answer me, or I'll think something is wrong."

Demons and saints... he's too close. His warm breath fans over my cheek.

I shrug him off and plant my palms on the cold stone to steady myself. *What did he ask?*

He reaches to the back of my head. I hiss from the contact that sends sharp pain searing across my skull.

When Cassius pulls his hand back, dark, glistening blood coats the tip of a finger.

"I'm sorry, little bird," he says, chagrined. "Let me heal that."

I block his hand away as he once again reaches for my wound. "No. I'm fine."

It's a lie. My head throbs and every word I speak sends more sharp needles of pain through my head.

Looking as if he's about to protest, I prepare for the pointless argument. We both know I will heal within the hour, but his offer would cut it down to only seconds.

To my surprise, Cassius clamps his mouth shut, pursing his lips. His eyes are downcast as he offers me a hand. I take it and let him help me up. Every muscle in my legs is weak.

"Please, Clara, allow me to heal you."

"I told you I was tired, but you didn't listen," I snap.

The pain only worsens my irritation. Even knowing it was an accident, I can't stop myself from taking my frustration out on him.

It's more than the stinging on the back of my head, more than the never ending training, more than the annoying conversation with that insufferable demon invading my mind, and more than long sleepless nights waiting for Alaric to tell me we will finally leave.

Cassius places a palm on the side of my face and runs his thumb under my eye. Whisps of pale hair have escaped the leather tie at the nape of his neck, making him appear uncharacteristically disheveled.

"You look like you haven't slept in days," he says quietly.

I grit my teeth, refusing to answer, refusing to tell him about Varin and their attempts to possess me in order to gain their freedom.

"Stop worrying about me. I just need space," I say, then walk out the door, closing it softly. To my surprise, Cassius doesn't try to stop me.

With each step, the pain in my head eases. There's a weird tingle and itching as the skin slowly knits back together—days of healing in minutes.

My gloomy mood hangs over me like a swirling storm cloud as I march down the hall, lost in thought. The scrape of a shoe on the stone pulls my attention to a tall figure descending the stairs.

He hesitates for a moment, then takes the last step and stops on the landing. I freeze, my breath hitching as the light from a sconce illuminates Alaric's face.

My pulse kicks up, roaring in my ears. I have only three options: walk past him, return to the training room and face Cassius, or take the stairs to the lower levels. None of them appeal to me.

The mark flares up in his presence, demanding I go to him. It's been almost two weeks since I last saw Alaric... since we fought and he sent me away. His cruel words still echo, cutting just as deep.

"Cassius wants you, Clara. Now go back to him."

"I don't want you. I never did."

When Alaric takes a step forward, I spin on my heel and run the other way. I don't make it far before he closes the distance with blinding speed. His arms encircle me from behind, pinning mine to my sides.

The familiarity of his touch is the comfort I crave as his warm, musky scent wraps around me. I sag against him. I don't have the energy to fight.

Alaric rests his cheek on my shoulder with a sigh. "I've missed you," he whispers. His embrace tightens, crushing my back against his muscular chest.

Why would he say that?

"I don't want you. I never did."

"I don't want you..."

Pressure builds behind my eyes, making my head throb. I squeeze my eyes shut and bite down on my bottom lip to keep from speaking.

Alaric inhales sharply and releases me without warning. He catches my shoulders as I stumble, then spins me to face him. It's even harder to look at him and be this close, knowing he chose to give me away.

His dark, sapphire eyes narrow when he catches the scent of blood. "You're hurt."

"It will heal soon enough," I say, shaking his hands off.

I am hurt. But not for the reason he's thinking. How can he act as if nothing happened—as if he didn't break me with his words? The expression he wears now is the same one that flickered in and out that night—the one that has made me doubt his harsh words.

Alaric's brow creases as he reaches for the back of my head. I push his arm away and take a step back. The hurt that's been festering for nearly two weeks gives way to anger. I want to know what changed and why.

"You've been avoiding me for over a week—you had to know I needed to talk. So why, after I've given up, are you here now?" I demand.

A dark look settles on his face. But before Alaric can answer, long fingers wrap around my upper arm and drag me back.

"Idiots," Cassius hisses, placing himself between us. "Both of you." He turns his icy glare on me, annoyance and disappointment written all over his features. He gives me a featherlight push toward the stairs. "Wait for me in your room."

And with that, I'm dismissed. My first instinct is to refuse—to stay and get the answers from Alaric now that he's in front of me.

The two of them stand perfectly still, glaring at each other, silently waiting for me to leave.

I trudge up the steps, dejected, the wounds across my heart bleeding and raw all over again. Asmod slithers along at my side, dutifully watching to ensure I do as my new master commands.

The second the two vampires are out of sight, Cassius's sharp words carry up to me. I pause to lift Asmod onto my shoulders, taking a moment to adjust their long body as I eavesdrop.

"You know better than to openly cross Elizabeth like this. What were you thinking, seeking her out like this?" I imagine Cassius rubbing his temples when he heaves an exasperated sigh.

Asmod bumps their nose against my cheek, nudging me to continue. Even though I want to hear more, I reluctantly start walking again.

"If someone saw and reported back to Elizabeth?" Cassius continues. "She expects me to oath bind Clara by…"

Wait…

Cassius was ordered to what?

I miss the rest of what he says when his voice trails off as I continue up the stairs.

Cassius was ordered to oath bind me... And not once has he uttered a single word about it. Head spinning wildly, I make my way to my room, fury coating my veins in ice.

CHAPTER TWO

CLARA

When Cassius saunters into my room, I fling my arm and release my grip. The dagger flies through the air and embeds into the door with a deep *thunk*.

A thin sliver of red beads up along the blade's path on his face. For several seconds, Cassius doesn't move, staring at me without blinking. Then slowly, he reaches up to touch his cheek. Pulling his hand away, he glares at the blood smeared on his fingertips.

"What in the Otherworld do you think you are doing?" he snarls. Ripping the dagger from the door, he crosses the small space in four long strides and drops it onto the table with a clatter.

"You bastard," I bite out, taking two steps forward, bringing us chest to chest, as we stare each other down. My breaths are quick and shallow, I'm hardly able to through my anger. "How dare you!"

"You know you can't be near him right now. Are you trying to get yourself killed?"

"This isn't about Alaric," I snap back.

Cassius's eyes widen as he takes me in. His hands come up to my shoulders and smooth up and down my arms in an effort to stop my trembling.

"Then what is this about?" Cassius asks gently. He reaches toward my head and sends a nasty glance toward Asmod, coiled up on my pillow. The demon's dark green metallic scales shimmer in the low evening light. "Are you still injured?"

I slap his hands away. "No, you demon's ass, this is about you keeping things from me—I heard you," I seethe. His eyes go wide, but I continue on before he can interrupt. "You want me to *trust* you when you hide things from me? Especially when they are rather important details—such as the fact that you are supposed to oath bind me to you!" My chest heaves with barely controlled fury.

"I was going—"

"No, you weren't." I plant both palms on his chest and shove him back a step. "You had more than enough chances, but you still kept me in the dark."

"If you're not going to breathe, will you please sit down before you pass out?"

I don't obey. He rolls his eyes in irritation and takes me by the shoulders, guiding me over to the only chair and sitting me down. When he's satisfied I won't stand back up, he retreats to the far wall. The distance takes some of the fuel from my burning anger.

"I will never let that happen," I say, hating how broken my voice comes out.

Cassius rubs his temples with his fingers and mutters something under his breath. Dropping his arms, he purses his lips. "As I was trying to say, I wanted to find a way around it before you found out. I knew you would sooner gut me than bind yourself to me."

I release a deep sigh, finally reining in my emotions.

Cassius takes a tentative step forward. When I don't protest or grab for the dagger to throw at his head again, he kneels and takes my hands in his.

"I have never marked a human, so I can't begin to understand what either of you are feeling, but I was trying to protect you."

It might be foolish, but I believe him. If he had any intention of following through, he would have done so by now.

"Keeping things from me for 'my protection' is

patronizing. I deserve to know anything that concerns me."

He nods and straightens to his feet. "You're right."

Taking several moments, I try to calm my body from the lingering effects of adrenaline and anger. "So, how can we keep this from happening? I don't want to be oath bound to you."

Cassius's eyes darken for a heartbeat. "That I have not been able to figure out quite yet. Elizabeth expects you to be oath bound to me as soon as possible. I told her I wanted your trust first instead of forcing it upon you. It's bought us a little time, but she is impatient."

I bite down on my bottom lip. "Can we… fake it?" I ask after a while, even knowing it's a terrible idea. Pretending to have Alaric's full mark didn't work, so I doubt something so much… bigger will.

"No," he says frankly, "but do not worry, little bird, we will figure something out."

I wake from a fitful sleep of tossing and turning. Stretching my legs out to ease cramped muscles, I instantly regret it as my feet slide against cold sheets.

Something unknown sends my heart racing, thudding almost painfully within my chest. My eyes snap open. Each exhalation of breath forms a white plume in front of me.

It's so cold—too cold to be natural.

A sliver of light cuts through the clouds and into the room. I keep as still as possible, scanning for anything out of place, anything that might have woken me. Slowly, I slide my hand under the pillow and wrap my half-frozen fingers around the hilt.

A small bowl rocks back and forth on the dresser.

Clara...

... Claraaa. They drag the sound of my name out, almost singing it.

I burrow deeper into my blankets as Varin's voice grows louder. More demanding. What does it say about me that I'm unbothered by a demon trying to worm their way into my mind while I sleep?

Though Varin visits almost every night, they never attack or harm me... just keep me awake with incessant pleadings to take the ring, to free them, to visit them. It's always the same conversation. The worst they've done so far is to slip into my mind and lead me down to their cell when I've been too exhausted to fight the compulsion.

"Damn you back to the Otherworld," I growl, cursing the demon.

Rolling back to my side, I settle in and pull the blanket over my shoulder, tucking it under my chin. Sleep calls to me almost as strongly as the demon does. Varin's taloned fingers scrape down my mental barrier, trying to break through. I shudder against each attempt.

The icy chill in the room remains as the long night wears on. Eventually, the demon stops pushing against my mind and retreats. The room warms, gradually relaxing my muscles, and I snuggle into the down pillow.

I try to push away all thoughts of the demon that have invaded my head all night and focus on Alaric. I remember the kiss we shared earlier and how the feel of his lips curled my toes… but the warmth they bring is doused like ice water on fire as the memory of being ripped from his arms plays over and over until irritation sets in.

It's a relief when my eyelids become heavy with sleep and slide closed.

Clara…

My name is a breath that echoes all around me, wrapping itself around my mind.

With a sharp inhale, I snap my eyes open. This time, the whispers are not in my head but come from every shadowy corner of the room.

Careful to keep still, I close my eyes and feign

sleep. Maybe if I ignore the pesky demon, they will go away and leave me to rest.

You are not sleeping. There is no use pretending. I hear your thoughts. The whisper is an icy breath against the side of my face. *Get up and come to my cell, Clara.*

I sit up, clutching the blanket to my chest. "Varin," I hiss. Their name forms as a small cloud from my lips.

Clara... Varin calls to me from the patch of impossibly thick darkness at the foot of my bed.

"Go away," I hiss and swat a hand in their direction. A shiver racks my entire body, starting from the base of my spine to the top.

A dark form takes shape from the shadows and slides across the bed. They can visit me at night, but their corporeal form is trapped in the forgotten cells deep in the bowels of the castle. "You need me, Clara."

"No, *you* need *me*," I snap irritably. "I know better than to make deals with demons."

A metal object clatters to the floor outside my room. Footsteps halt abruptly.

I go still, hoping whoever is out there didn't overhear me talking. The sigh of power coming from Varin makes the fine hairs on the back of my neck stand on end.

I can help you... I can help you be with your beloved vampire again.

My heart pounds against the wall of my chest.

It *is* tempting.

It would mean I wouldn't be forced to oath bind myself to Cassius, and Alaric would be free of the queen…

Varin chuckles inside my mind.

Demon shit. With the mere suggestion that I could leave this place with Alaric, they managed to slip past my guard.

Gritting my teeth, I force the demon out.

I sag in relief and fight against the tide of disappointment that threatens to drown me. The offer is tempting… or it would be if it didn't mean allowing a demon to possess me.

Even if we agreed to a single action, a single moment, I doubt Varin would relinquish control over my body so easily.

And I will be damned to the Otherworld before I willingly free them from their shackles.

It's still dark outside, but the first chirps of morning birds sound through my window. I collapse back onto my pillow and drop my arm over my eyes.

The day hasn't even started yet, and I am already exhausted.

CHAPTER THREE

CLARA

I peel my eyes open to a stream of warm light streaming in through the window. My pulse leaps in my throat. Jolting upright, I rub the sleep from my eyes as it registers that I've slept in—by a lot.

After Varin's power weakened and they finally released their talons from my unconscious mind, I slept like the dead.

I scan the room, looking for anything out of place, but it is exactly the same as it was last night.

As much as I long to lie back down and sleep for a few more hours, I know it's pointless. Cassius never lets me shirk training. While he hasn't come to fetch me yet, that doesn't mean he won't.

I fling the blankets off and climb out of bed to prepare for the day's training. Minutes later, I am dressed in soft leather leggings, broken-in knee-high boots, and a simple tunic with a loose collar tucked in at the waist.

I'm in the middle of braiding my hair when the door opens.

"I'm almost rea—" I turn, and the words die on my tongue when I see Cassius's grave expression. "What happened?"

He closes the door quietly and crosses to me. The silence stretches on so long that my skin itches from the anticipation.

Asmod lifts their head from Cassius's shoulder and looks at me with dark red eyes, then slithers to the ground, gliding across the room. There's a light rustle of fabric as the demon settles into blankets on the bed.

Ever since my confrontation with Alexander, the demon snake has found their way into my room and shown up during training, more and more often.

"Say something," I beg, swallowing hard, "or I'm going to think you're not here to give me the day off after all." My attempt at lightening the mood fails miserably.

Cassius shakes his head, averting his gaze. "There is a change in plans for the day," he starts slowly as if he must physically pull each word from his tongue. "The queen has an announcement to make."

They aren't words that would inspire dread—but this is Elizabeth—and Cassius's reaction can only mean that whatever it is, it won't be good.

Nothing has happened yet, and there is no reason to worry until something does. I bite down hard on my lip and remind myself not to overreact.

It's an announcement. Nothing more, nothing less.

"Hurry and change your clothes. We cannot have you standing before her looking like that."

"What are you not saying?" I demand.

He tsks, openly unhappy about my insistence. "The queen wants you presentable. Now strip. We don't have much time."

Demons and saints—presentable for what? My stomach churns.

Elizabeth has ordered me to be presentable, which can only be for one or two reasons—either Alaric or her patience has run out because Cassius has not oath bound me to him yet.

Cassius kneels before my trunk and pulls out a dark gray dress. It's simple, with frayed lace embellishments along the curve of my hips and around the deep neckline. The material is light and looks as if it were made from ash. Somehow, that seems fitting.

He pools the dress on the floor at my side, allowing me to sidestep into it easily. I motion for him to look away before turning my back on him to remove my training clothes.

The material is silky against my skin. Unfortunately, I'll still need his help with the complicated lacing up the back.

"You can turn back around now," I say, clutching the dress to my chest."

His hands work the laces, tying them with deft efficiency, pausing halfway to move my partially braided hair over my shoulder. His knuckles brush my skin lightly, pausing for a heartbeat before resuming the task of lacing me up.

When he's finished, Cassius runs his fingers through my hair, unbraiding it and working out all the knots I neglected to brush when I was initially getting ready. I appreciate that he doesn't tie it into the uncomfortable styles that are popular with the court but instead allows it to remain down, as I prefer to wear it. I will be the only one with my hair not styled, but I won't stick out any more than the queen intends anyway.

Cassius turns me to face him, but after a second of his pitying gaze, I avert my eyes.

I get the impression this announcement is largely to put me in my place and remind me, in some unpleasant manner, that she is the one with power.

My hand skims over my stomach, where

Alexander opened me up with his nails. As if I could forget that most see me as nothing more than a human whose use barely extends beyond being a food source.

Cassius slides a hand down the length of my arm, gliding over the faint scars to tangle his fingers in mine. He tries to smile, but it falls as quickly as it appears.

It feels intimate. I tug once on my arm, but he tightens his grip. Too nervous to fight over something so meaningless, I stop resisting.

Several minutes pass with us standing in my room, holding hands. I stare at a spot on the wall until my gaze blurs. The weight of his eyes on me is heavy. Cassius gives my hand a gentle squeeze, drawing my attention back to him.

I scrunch my brows in silent question. His mouth is drawn in a tight line, and his brows pull together in pity. Cassius lowers his eyes in a slow blink, like a subtle bow. The gesture seems to say *everything will be all right*.

Nerves prickle under my skin as we wait and wait and wait.

The clocktower bell in town rings, echoing through the air. It's early evening. I must have slept most of the day away without realizing it.

Cassius tucks my arm under his, then escorts me

from the room. We walk with an even pace that is just this side of too slow. The only sound as we make our way through the corridors is that of our footsteps.

We are the last to arrive.

Vampires fill the throne room. There are more here today than during the ball. Scanning the area, I don't see another human among the masses.

Cassius pulls me tighter into his side and slinks along the back wall with me in tow.

Letting him guide the way, I stretch my neck, rising up on my toes to try and find Alaric. I know he's here because I can feel him through the mark. He calls to me the closer he is. Too distracted after yesterday's training session, I failed to sense him, but now, his pull on our strange connection is nearly tangible.

A large hand lands on my shoulder and pushes me down. Cassius frowns, shaking his head followed by a quick jerk of his chin in the queen's direction.

Demon shit.

Her cold lavender eyes root me in place as she leans over the arm of her throne to whisper to a guard. He nods sharply, then begins walking in our direction.

I take a step back to hide behind Cassius, trying desperately to disappear.

His fingers wrap around my upper arms before

I'm halfway there. "It is too late now, little bird. You cannot fly away this time."

The crowd parts to let the guard through. Crimson ringed eyes lock onto my face. He stops several feet away. "Come with me," he says in a clipped tone.

I swallow the lump of fear that forms in my throat, and after a last furtive glance at Cassius, I follow the guard toward the front. I'm grateful when Cassius stays with me, his hand on my back to guide me. The vampire crowd closes in behind us as we pass like a wave of water that wants to pull us under.

Once we are in front, Elizabeth stands. She is alone. Sheer lace runs through the black dress fitted to her slender and lithe form. It hugs her arms and wends around her ribs, over her stomach and hips, to the high slit on one leg. The long skirt trails behind her.

A light tug on my heart turns my stomach into knots. I hold my breath. Alaric is close, I feel him, and not for the first time, I wish we could communicate through the mark.

Under the bone-white crown with its thick, jutting points, her golden hair is pinned up in intricate twists and knots, ending in a cascade of curls down her back.

Elizabeth glares openly at me, and even though I

know I shouldn't meet her gaze, I can't help myself. The corner of her mouth ticks up as she lifts her arm and turns to the side. I follow the movement.

Alaric emerges from the back and steps up to her side. My heart aches when he slips his hand into hers and doesn't let go.

"In two months' time, our prince will take his rightful place at my side." Elizabeth glances at him, giving him a falsely warm smile. "He will be crowned, and then oath bound to me."

I gasp before I can stop myself at the same time the crowd breaks out in mild applause.

The queen's sharp gaze cuts to me. Her mouth lifts into a smug expression, eyes dancing with hate.

Alaric lifts her hand and lowers his face to her palm. Her mouth forms a small O.

When he speaks, it's quiet, but I'm close enough to just make out the words. "We all do what we must for the ones we love."

Alaric presses a soft kiss to her knuckles then lifts his head to gaze adoringly into her eyes. The world shifts under my feet. I must sway because Cassius tucks me into his side.

I'm losing him...

His deep, sapphire blue eyes are clear and bright as he turns from Elizabeth and looks out over the crowd. Alaric's gaze pauses on me for a painful heartbeat before moving on. The din of voices and clapping fade to a quiet hum beneath the buzzing in my head. There is no spark of red, no dullness, no strain that suggests that she's compelling him into compliance. He is walking into this willingly.

Two months...

Two months until he will be crowned as Elizabeth's consort. I knew he would eventually be crowned, but I hadn't expected it to be so soon.

And to agree to oath bind himself to her—to the woman he loathes more than anything in this world— with a smile on his face?

Cassius's arm tightens around me.

He knew about this.

He knew—and he kept it from me even after he promised to stop hiding things.

Fissures crack over the surface of my heart. My breath comes in short, shallow bursts until spots form across my vision, dancing until all I can see is Alaric's face and the loving way he gazes at her.

CHAPTER FOUR

CLARA

WE ALL DO WHAT WE MUST FOR THE ONES WE LOVE.

The scene repeats over and over in my mind. My words... He used *my* words... for *her*. It's petty because they are only words, but it feels like a betrayal.

Alaric gazed at her with genuine feeling. It looked too real for it not to be. Thinking about it twists my stomach into knots. I couldn't even make it to training before the wave of emotions overwhelmed me: anger, confusion, hurt... and pride.

Now I find myself down the hall from the training room, unable to go any farther. Hiding in the shadows, like a coward, I press my back against the cold stone, as if I could become part of it.

I press the heel of my hands into my eyes until I

see stars, attempting to stifle the burn and ache behind my eyes. The last thing I need right now is for Cassius to see me cry. I'm not sure I could stand to see pity and judgment when he looks at me.

Cassius refused to give me the day off, even after what happened. No. It was back to my room to change and an order to be down in the training room within the hour.

Biting down on my lip, I lean against the wall as the pressure building behind my eyes continues to grow. I press my palms to my cheeks and tilt my head back. But it doesn't matter, the second I blink, two thick tears slide down my cheeks. I roughly swipe at them with my sleeve.

Yesterday, Alaric held me and said he missed me after avoiding me for almost two weeks. His actions contradict themselves, and I don't know what is real and what isn't.

Footsteps descend the stairs above me. I cover my mouth to stifle the sound of my breathing and crouch low.

The man pauses at the bottom for several heartbeats before he continues walking. My heart pounds as his back comes into view. I would recognize him and the way he moves even in the dark.

For the second time in as many days, Alaric has

passed me in this hall. If I'm ever going to get answers from him, it needs to be now because I don't know if I'll ever get another chance.

Resisting the urge to run after him, I wait until he's farther down the hall before following outside of the torchlight.

He either doesn't notice or doesn't care.

Alaric passes the training room and continues to the end of the hall. He extinguishes the torch then turns the corner, moving quietly down the stairs.

I curse inwardly. He might not need light, but my human eyes do.

Placing my palm against the wall, I speed up in an attempt to close the distance. Acrid smoke hangs in the air from the extinguished torch, burning my nostrils.

When my fingers find the corner, I pause to listen. There is only the sound of my pulse thrumming through my veins.

Demons and saints, I've lost him. He's probably already at the bottom and through the door. I turn the corner and descend anyway.

After a dozen steps, I collide with a solid form, losing my balance from the unexpected impact. My heart stops for two beats before restarting and drumming at twice the normal speed. Strong hands grip my upper arms, steadying me.

"What are you doing here, Clara?" Alaric demands.

I pull back, tilting my head up as if I could see his face in the pitch dark. "I was following you."

He grunts. "I can see that. But *why?*"

The coldness of his question stings. "I want to talk to you…" I croak. "Do I really need a reason?"

He's silent for a moment. Then he shifts me so my back is to the wall and leans in, brushing his lips against the shell of my ear. "Quiet," he whispers.

I strain to hear what he does, but my human ears aren't good enough. Keeping still, I close my eyes and imagine we are anywhere else.

My little fantasy shatters moments later when he shifts, placing his hands against the wall on either side of my head, pinning me into place. I long to reach for him, to feel his arms wrap around me.

He tilts his head so his lips come to rest lightly against my cheek. "You can't seek me out again, Clara. I am to be crowned and oath bound by the queen."

"I know," I snap. "It seems everyone knew except for me. Cassius knew and kept it from me—"

"He was ordered not to say anything, so don't be too angry with him."

I can't help the choking sound that works free. My heart feels like glass shattering on stone. I press my hands against his chest, then shove him back a step.

"I don't understand you, Alaric. How can you tell me not to look for you, after yesterday?"

A thick silence hangs between us.

"That was a mistake," he says eventually. His voice is barely above a whisper, but the words ring in my ears.

"Why did you bring me here? I came because I didn't want to be trapped, and you let me." Shaking my head, I continue before he can interrupt. "You play her games, and I am the pawn in the center of it all. I've been thrown in the dungeon, marked, given away. You tell me you'll return, then with your next breath you say you never wanted me. You avoided me only to chase me down and say you missed me, and now..."

Cutting off my incoherent rambling, I swipe at the tears streaming down my cheeks. I'm too upset to organize my thoughts.

He says nothing as I work to regain control of my emotions. Alaric leans on the wall, hands pressed to the stone on either side of my head.

"You are inconsistent, and I can't tell what is real anymore. Everything you do ends up hurting me," I say. The sound of his breathing is the only hint that I'm not alone. "Tell me to accept Cassius as my new master and give up on you for good."

"No." The word is harsh and sharp, but he softens against me.

"Why?" My voice cracks.

Then his hands are on my face, thumbs swiping at the tears. Alaric brings his face down and rests his forehead against mine. "Because, my dear Clara," he starts slowly, "you are in my blood and in my bones and… I am in love with you."

My heart does a flip.

"When I am cold to you, it is to protect you." He kisses my right eye. "When I look for you, when I touch you, it is because I am weak and selfish." He places a kiss on my other eye. "I know I should stay away—and I try—but your very essence calls to me, driving me mad until all reason is gone, and I can no longer fight it. Your existence makes me reckless."

His admission startles me. I wait for a reaction, but all I feel is hurt and anger.

I slide sideways against the wall and move up a step. Then another. Alaric lets his hands fall away.

"You are cruel," I hiss.

"Clara…" His voice is raw.

I shake my head again. *This isn't love. It can't be.* I thought my heart had shattered—but this is a knife to my chest, intent on finishing the job.

"You don't hurt the ones you love," I say.

Then I turn and run. I don't slow until I reach my room. My shaking fingers fumble with the latch. Only when I'm inside, with my back pressed against the warped wood door, do I allow the tears to fall in earnest.

Alaric doesn't follow

I hate this. I hate that he said that. I hate that all I can seem to do is cry. It makes me feel weak and pathetic.

A hiccup that is part sob and part laughter bubbles up. *Who would have ever thought that I would cry over a vampire?*

When the tears subside, and I'm cold from sitting on the floor, I stand and cross to the dresser. I pour water from the carafe into a small wooden bowl, then splash my face until my skin is no longer overheated.

Water clings to my lashes and dribbles down my neck. I feel around for a towel when there's a soft knock.

Growling, I wipe my sleeve over my face. I'm not in the mood for Cassius or his training. He will give me the day off; it won't change anything in the end.

More than ready to deliver a tongue lashing, I jerk open the door, then freeze with my mouth hanging open.

Alaric stands inches in front of me, lashes clinging together in thick clumps. I grip the edge of the door and prepare to close it. I don't have it in me to continue our conversation.

A single heartbeat later, his arms band around me, lifting me up into a tight hug. Alaric steps inside and kicks the door shut with his booted foot. He lowers me back down, but he doesn't let go.

Alaric nestles his face in the crook of my neck. "I love you," he breathes against my skin.

Reaching up, I place my hands on his chest and push. He doesn't budge under my human strength.

"I never wanted to hurt you, but I will continue to do so if it means keeping you alive and safe." A deep, shuddering sigh rolls through him. "Even if it means you end up hating me—I will never stop loving you."

My arms go limp, and I press my cheek against his muscular chest, inhaling his musky scent. I search for the lie among his words or deception in the way he holds me, but I can find none.

We remain like this for several long minutes. Eventually, Alaric loosens his hold and ducks his head to look me in the eye. "I don't know how to do this, to play the part Elizabeth demands while staying true to myself and to you."

If I were smart, I would call him a liar regardless of what my heart wants. If I were smart, I would send him away.

But I'm not...

And I cannot help but believe him.

The truth winds itself around my heart, and I can't ignore it. There is reason behind each and every contradiction.

Throat thick with lingering hurt and mixed with understanding, I nod. Then I realize he hasn't asked me anything, but it's all I can manage.

Ever since he gave me the first mark, I've been afraid of losing myself and him… and these emotions. There's still so much I don't know or understand about the mark and how it connects us.

I take two deep breaths as I back up. I push everything down and say the first thing that comes to mind. "Why did you say *that* to her during the announcement?"

Alaric tugs a hand through his hair and huffs out a laugh. "I may have been looking at her, but I was talking to you."

"Oh." It's a silly thing, but it makes a difference. Then something occurs to me. "Why couldn't I feel you coming down the stairs? I could feel you during…"

"It only works when you actively seek me out or call to me," he says simply, then adds, "I truly am sorry, my dear Clara, for everything."

My heart thunders in my chest. Suddenly nervous, I chew on the inside of my cheek and search for anything else to talk about, something lighter, easier—

Alaric dips his head, tangling his fingers in my hair as his mouth crashes down on mine. It only takes a fraction of a second for me to melt into him. His lips move over mine, firm and demanding. Hungry. Opening up to him, his tongue dances across mine, fangs scraping against my bottom lip. I push up on my toes, deepening the kiss, but he breaks it all too soon.

An apology, a declaration of love, and a kiss are not enough to fix things between us.

But it is a step in the right direction.

The pain his words and actions caused will not disappear, but I can forgive him and focus on the present so we can move forward together.

"We better get you to training before Cassius comes looking for you. I doubt he'll be pleased to find me in your room."

I flatten my heels and sigh. He's right, but there's so much left unsaid, so many questions, so many things to figure out, and so much to say.

Except, all I can think of is that Alaric loves me even when he had every reason not to.

Past the pain and our glaring imperfections, despite how the world tries to keep us apart, somehow, we have found our way to each other.

CHAPTER FIVE

CLARA

MY EYES FLY OPEN AT THE SOUND OF MY NAME. My first instinct is to curse Varin for denying me sleep a second night in a row.

"Clara," Alaric says, closer than before.

I lift my head and find his face barely an inch from mine.

"What are you doing here?" Furrowing my brow, I sit up and rub my eyes.

Alaric takes my hand, palm up in his. He runs a fingertip over the sensitive skin, slowly tracing the lines.

Cupping his cheek, I ask, "Did something happen?"

"No. I've come to ask you something—it's reckless

and most definitely a terrible idea," he says without lifting his gaze.

My mind whirls with possibilities. "Ask me."

"I would like to take you somewhere for a few hours. I will have you back with enough time to get plenty of sleep."

"Yes," I say without hesitation.

His head snaps up, and he smiles broadly as if he expected me to refuse. But the truth is, he could ask me for anything, and I would always say yes.

Rising from the bed, I dress quickly and cross the room to where Alaric awaits near the door.

"I'm ready," I say.

He slips an arm around my waist and pulls me in for a kiss. If he wanted to change plans and stay, I wouldn't complain.

After several exquisite moments, he pulls away and takes my hand in his again as if by habit before he leads me out into the hall. We hurry through the narrow back passages, ducking into empty rooms or dark corners when anyone draws near. The hallways are nearly empty as some humans retire for the night while others rise for the night to pamper and serve the court.

The cold winter air takes my breath away as we step out into the night. Alaric tucks me into his side as a shiver skates over my body.

I glance up at him in awe. We are so far from where we started.

It almost doesn't feel real.

He loves me.

Again, emotions rise, threatening to overwhelm me and I have to clear my throat to speak. "Where are we going?"

Pressing a finger to his mouth, he tilts his head toward the stable. We move silently, crossing the grounds, not even talking once we enter the building.

Alaric leads the way, stopping at the second to last stall where a large black horse with a white blaze on its face. The same one we rode together at Windbury when we thought we could fool everyone into believing he marked me.

He opens the stall door, and the horse walks out, stopping in the center of the aisle, obeying a silent command.

My pulse races, and I bite down hard on my lip to keep from asking questions.

Without a saddle or bridle, Alaric leaps gracefully onto the animal. He leans forward, offering me a hand, and pulls me up in front of him. One arm wraps tightly around my waist. His other grips the mane. Then we're off. I let out a surprised squeak, clasping my hands over my mouth.

Within minutes, we are riding down a side road away from the castle and the city.

"Are we leaving?" I ask, hopeful even though he said a few hours.

His fingers flex, pressing into my hip. "No," he says.

Disappointment silences all other thoughts.

We ride for what feels like an hour before stopping near a rocky area. Trees sprout between rocks, roots clinging to them as they would dirt and wedging themselves in the deep crevices. Water from a stream or river burbles soothingly somewhere nearby.

"Will there be any demons out here?" I ask as Alaric dismounts behind me.

"No, there are far too many vampires in Nightwich for them to bother haunting these lands."

He grips my waist and lifts me. Bracing my hands on his shoulders, he gently lowers me to the ground. I step sideways and drink in our surroundings.

It's beautiful. My mouth drops open as I take in the thick cover of trees to the east, the tall, looming peaks of the mountains to the far west, and the endless black sky filled with infinite stars that glitter like broken glass overhead. The night is clear without a cloud in sight. I've never dreamed of standing out in the open after sunset, far away from shelter and without fear of demons.

Wood smoke brings my attention back to Alaric. He crouches around a pile of stones and sticks, building a small fire. Flames catch with a whoosh.

Another shiver skitters over me, and I hurry to join him at the fire. Alaric's arm snakes around my waist and pulls me closer. The warmth of his body is more comforting than the fire. Resting my head on his shoulder, I close my eyes, wishing this could last forever.

"How are you?" Alaric asks tentatively.

Pressing a hand against his chest, I lean back and frown. "I am all right," I say slowly, then ask, "What do you mean?"

He twists to look me in the eyes. "Your mother… It's been a week, and you haven't said a word."

Oh.

That.

"How did you find out?" I ask, digging at the dirt with a finger. I take a deep breath and think for a moment, afraid that if he finds me cold and callous, he'll want to take back his earlier words.

"Cassius told me."

Of course he did.

"I… I am numb to it," I say honestly, peeking up at him through my lashes and expecting a look of disgust or disapproval. But his features remain neutral, so I go on. "I don't know if what happened hasn't hit me yet. For most of my life I believed she was already dead—I've been mourning her since I was eight." I pause to take a breath, then continue as I twist and untwist the edge of my sleeve around a finger. "The woman I met here was nothing like the mother I knew. It's almost as if nothing changed... This version of her was a stranger with a familiar face."

When I finally stop talking, a heavy silence settles between us. The fire snaps, and a piece of wood shifts, sending embers into the air that fade against the night sky.

Holding my breath, I wait for him to hate me for not feeling as I should, for being heartless and unworthy of his affection.

"I understand," he says.

I release a sigh, grateful that he hasn't condemned me. Wanting to move the conversation to anything else, I turn the question back on him. "How are you doing... with Elizabeth's demands?"

The deep, blue sapphire of his irises darkens to nearly black. "I hate every hour of it, loathe every minute I'm forced to be at her side, and despise every second I am away from you." The vampire at my side shrinks in on himself. "I can feel my freedom slipping away every night. It's the one thing I've always feared."

The dread and desperation of his impending fate weigh heavy on his shoulders.

Guilt settles like a rock in my gut. I am responsible for *all of this*.

I took his sister's life, and he claimed me in exchange for the life debt I owe. Then when the queen found out, she ordered him to Nightwich. Returning to Windbury after Kitty's wedding and coming here with him have all led to a gilded cage forming around him, one bar at a time. And in two months, the door will clang shut, locking him away for good.

Demon shit, I have ruined his life in every way possible. It's my fault he will be oath bound to Elizabeth. I don't understand how he can stand being in my company, let alone believe that he loves me.

My heart and head war with each other, one believing his words, the other incapable.

"Clara? What's wrong?" he asks, cutting through my thoughts.

"I have ruined your life," I say. His brows shoot up. "If it wasn't for me, you wouldn't have claimed—"

"You can't take responsibility for my actions." He twists to look me in the eye, gripping my chin between his thumb and forefinger and pointing in the direction of Nightwich with his other hand. "Or Elizabeth's... or anyone else's for that matter. We are all responsible for our choices and how we react to the those around us. No one makes us do anything."

I bite down on the inside of my cheek. His thumb brushes back and forth over my bottom lip.

"I would have ended up here eventually." He gives me a joyless half-smile. "It's horrible and I shouldn't be, but I am glad that you are with me."

He lists his head to the side, dark eyes glittering like they hold the night sky. I want his love, and I will do anything I can to keep it, even if I don't deserve it after everything I've done.

Rising to my knees, I throw my arms around his neck. Unprepared, he topples over, landing on his back, taking me with him.

"If I was stronger, I could fix this..." I whisper, resting my cheek on his chest. "I could save you."

Alaric moves a hand up and down my back in soothing strokes. "You are the strongest person I know—human or vampire."

I lift my head to find him smiling, the barest glimpse of his fangs peeking out. *Demons and saints, how can he smile right now?*

"If I could just stay by your side, I could fix this," I insist.

"Don't put all of this on your shoulders, my dear

Clara. It is not your place to change fate." Alaric rolls to the side so we lay facing each other. Reaching up, his fingers glide over my temple, pushing a strand of hair behind my ear.

He's wrong. He keeps saying it's not my fault, not my responsibility, but I can't silence the voice that says otherwise.

I clutch at the front of his shirt, pulling myself closer. "If I were a vampire, I would be strong enough."

"No." The word cuts through the air between us, sharp and inflexible.

Stilling, I hold my breath against the bitter disappointment. I should have expected that. My hands fall away from his shirt, and I push up to sit.

"Clara—"

"I'm cold." I scoot away from him and inch closer to the fire, hugging my knees to my chest.

He shifts, but I keep my gaze locked on the dancing flames, blinding me to everything else. The wood crackles and pops gently.

"It's not for the reasons you assume."

"How do you know what I'm thinking?" I ask harsher than I mean to.

He chuckles. "Because I know you better than you realize."

Alaric shifts again, cradling my hips with his legs

as he settles behind me. Two strong arms envelop me, pulling my back against his chest. I don't fight his embrace—I don't want to.

He sighs and rests his cheek on the top of my head. "I did horrible things in my past that I don't want you to experience… and I don't want you to find out what a monster I truly am."

My stomach churns. *I called him a monster once.* It couldn't be further from the truth, but he believes it is. If I had known, would I have still said it to him?

The truth is shame churning my insides. At the time, I would have. In fact, I would have used it against him at every opportunity. My hate for *what* he is would have blinded me to *who* he really is.

No matter what we wish, the past is set in stone. We are powerless to change it, but we can learn from it.

"Why?" I ask.

"Because you will hate me."

"Aren't we a pair?" I run a finger along the hand that rests on my knee. "We are both afraid of the same thing."

"I told you I would never stop—"

"I am still afraid," I interrupt. Fear and insecurity are irrational things that defy the heart and mind. Not used to those emotions, I don't know how to deal with them.

"Cassius is supposed to oath bind me to him."

Alaric stiffens at my back at the abrupt change in subject.

"If I were a vampire," I continue, "then he wouldn't need to and—"

Alaric sighs wearily. "I can see you're not about to give in."

I don't even know if I would want to become a vampire… but if it meant not being oath bound to Cassius and having the strength so I could help Alaric, I would be willing to risk it.

Twisting awkwardly to face him, I'm met with sorrowful eyes and a deep frown. A moment ago, I wondered if it could be a viable solution to some of our problems.

"I will not turn you. But if I tell you what I did, then will you promise to drop this?"

I nod solemnly and face forward, leaning back against him.

Alaric drops his forehead to my shoulder. His pain is palpable, and that's all I need to change my mind. The details don't matter because no one hurts this much over something small.

"No, Alaric, you don't have to tell me. I won't ask again."

He presses his lips just below my ear in a sweet kiss, and then he begins. "After Elizabeth first turned me, I was angry at the world. She used Rosalie to get to me. My first night, she brought me two humans, and I killed them—I didn't intend to—but at the time, I didn't understand what was happening. It seemed impossible, after all, vampires were nothing more than stories told to children so they would behave."

His arms shake around me from the rage his memories dredge up. I thread my fingers through his and bring his hand to my lips to kiss his palm. It's the only thing I can think to do.

The words that would make this all right for him don't exist. All I have to give is comfort with small touches and gestures, never letting go.

It seems to help.

"Those deaths only fueled my anger, and the next night, I went out to a tavern I used to frequent when I was still human... I had one too many drinks, and when I woke up several hours later..." His voice grows pained as he speaks. "I had slaughtered them all —friends and neighbors I grew up with, people I knew since I was a child. I would have ended my life then and there if it hadn't been for Rosalie. I stayed to protect her, and in return, she somehow helped me reclaim the scraps of my humanity."

Alaric falls silent and sags against me, face pressed to my neck. His arms tighten, crushing me to his chest. Ragged breaths are warm through my clothing. I swallow thickly.

My gentle vampire just admitted to acts I never thought possible by his hand. I would expect similar from most other vampires—but never him.

I pull his arms tighter around me and squeeze. He feels the pain and regret of his actions after all this time. My heart aches for him and the pain he carries that has never faded.

It must have been a very long time ago because no one in Littlemire has ever spoken of such a massacre. If it were to happen today, every known town would know about it within a month, and the stories would linger for decades.

"I understand," I say. Twisting to sit with my side against him, I place a kiss on the corner of his mouth. His eyes slide closed as he leans into the gesture.

Alaric clears his throat and offers a half-hearted smile.

"When you are oath bound to her, what will become of the mark?" I ask after a while.

"It will dissolve, and you will be free." He tries to sound upbeat, hopeful, but there is a note of something darker and jagged in his tone.

My heart thuds painfully.

Free.

That word has changed meaning so many times I

no longer recognize it. Not having the mark will not make me free. It will feel confining. Empty.

"I will never let her oath bind you. I will protect you," I say, "like you've protected me."

Alaric chuckles but not unkindly. "I don't doubt that." He kisses me. "But you must never forget that you are human in a world of vampires." The smile falls from his lips. "She won't hesitate to kill you if you try."

"Being tied to her will kill *you*," I shoot back.

He shrugs one shoulder. "I do not care if she ends my life. I do not wish to live in a world that you are not part of."

"How can you speak so casually of your own death?"

"When you have forever stretched out ahead of you and have lived several lifetimes, there is very little to distinguish the two."

I furrow my brows, not understanding how anyone could feel that way. But that is impossible because I will never have that amount of time.

He may not believe a human can protect a vampire against the most powerful of them—and maybe he's right—but he has given me his heart and stolen mine.

I refuse to let him resign to this fate. Inhaling, I'm ready to say as much when he speaks up before I get the chance.

"We should get going if I am to return you to your room with enough time to sleep. I doubt Cassius will go easy on you in training." He runs a hand through his hair.

Even though a big part of me wants to beg him for more time, I know he's right. Cassius was furious with me today when I was not only late to training but tired and distracted as well. My efforts were abysmal.

When Alaric woke me, wanting to take me somewhere, this hadn't been what I expected, but it was what I needed, and I think he did too—even if it wasn't nearly long enough.

We enter the castle the same way we left. There is more activity now, so it's harder to remain inconspicuous, and Alaric has to compel several of them into forgetting they've seen us. It would be safer for us to part ways immediately, but he insists on escorting me all the way to my room.

A hand latches onto my arm, yanking me back into the shadows of an alcove. My shoulder hurts, as if the limb was nearly ripped off. I reach for the hilt of the dagger, freezing with the blade half drawn at the murderous look on Cassius's slender, handsome face. The sharp angle of light and dark playing on his features makes him appear feral.

He snarls low in his chest, shoving me behind him. My back hits the wall, forcing the air from my lungs as Alaric reaches us, fangs bared. Thick red rings of demon-sent power nearly swallow the blue of his eyes.

"Who do you think you are touching her?" he growls.

"Have the two of you completely taken leave of your senses?" Cassius returns the snarl. "I am her master now, not you. She will be oath bound to me once you are bound to Elizabeth." He delivers the words coldly, wrapping his fingers around my arm to keep me in place.

I struggle against his iron grip, stopping when I realize I'm only hurting myself.

"I have marked her—"

"And you will lose her forever if you do not leave," Cassius interrupts. "*Now.*" The fierceness drops from Alaric's face. "For her... Leave for her. You don't know her anymore."

My throat is tight and parched. I've stopped breathing, waiting for Alaric's protest.

He meets my gaze for only an instant before

returning his attention to Cassius. With a terse nod, he turns on his heel and leaves. My heart cracks as Alaric disappears from view

Cassius finally releases my arm. This is for the best right now, at least until I figure out how to fix things.

And I will.

You don't know her anymore.

This is a temporary setback, but that doesn't stop the separation from hurting or keep me from hating Cassius for his words and for his part in all of this.

CHAPTER SIX

CLARA

Sitting back against the stone wall of my room, I cross my legs and rest my book in my lap. I run my hand over the faded title. The familiar scent of parchment and leather is comforting. A candelabrum sits on the wood post of the bed, providing me with just enough light to read. Sleep refused to come after the events of last night and the previous day.

I open the book to the first page and stare blankly at the words on the page. Two sentences in, and my mind has already wandered back to Alaric's words. *I will never stop loving you.*

He loves me. The proclamation swells in my heart. It's almost enough of a balm to ease my irritation at Cassius for sending him away.

I still fear losing Alaric, but I no longer doubt him.

He will do what is necessary, as will I. This kind of love is foreign to me. Nothing Xander and I ever shared ever came close to this.

Pounding on my door startles me from my thoughts. My smile fades as a servant walks in.

"I have been sent to fetch you, Miss Valmont. We are to begin preparing you for the upcoming coronation."

My mood is instantly soured. I close the book with a snap, blowing out the candle as I stand. There's no point in arguing. Besides, I must prove myself to be the perfect human pet.

The woman scans me from head to toe, pulling a face. I'm still wearing the deerskin leggings and tucked-in shirt from the outing with Alaric.

I follow her to a new area of the castle I haven't been to before, located close to the court member's quarters. She opens the door to a room at the end of the hall and gestures for me to enter. The door clicks shut behind me.

A woman sits at a table, hunched over a book, furiously writing. The scratching of her quill halts as she looks up from her work.

"Don't just stand there," she says, waving a hand at the circular fitting platform in the center of the room.

I step up, and in seconds, the seamstress is at my

back, taking my measurements, lifting my arms in a quick, efficient movement as if I were a mannequin.

She hums, stepping back, eyes assessing me before scribbling something down a ledger. I mentally prepare for several long hours of standing in the same spot and being poked and prodded with needles every time I dare fidget or move too much.

"Don't move. I will be right back," the seamstress says in a clipped tone before striding from the room.

I let my arms fall to my sides. Several minutes pass, and when the woman doesn't return, I decide to risk her annoyance and explore the room.

Three folding screens line the wall to the right, one in each corner and one in the center. A long table set against the wall opposite the door holds mounds of cloth in every color and texture imaginable.

Everything in the room is the shades of cream—from the light ash wood furniture and accents to the pale sand floor stones. Floor-to-ceiling leaded windows partially hidden by thick, ivory curtains span almost the entire length of the left wall, with two small, round tables stationed in front.

I make my way to the long table and run my hand along the assortment of fabrics. Some are thick, others partially transparent, with tulle and lace mixed in.

The door opens. I spin and snatch my hand away

from the expensive materials, prepared to mutter a halfhearted apology. But it's not the seamstress who walks through the door, and the words die on my tongue before I can even breathe.

Swathed in dark shades of purple, the vampire queen glides into the room, her royal mantel flowing out in her wake. The gown is like a second skin, hugging her from the high collar down and flaring out at mid-thigh.

"Hello, Miss Valmont. I was hoping we could have a chat."

I can't say no, but she doesn't need my permission.

Elizabeth takes my silence as an answer. She walks to one of the round tables and runs a long, thin finger over the surface. She frowns but takes a seat anyway. Every move and gesture is eerily graceful.

She flicks her wrist, and the servant waiting next to the door snaps to attention.

"Tea," she says, not taking her eyes off me. "Come, Clara, we have much to talk about." Elizabeth motions to the chair opposite her.

I snap my mouth shut and cross the room on weak legs. Elizabeth watches my approach with the razor-sharp gaze of a predator, searching for any weakness. Gripping onto the back of the chair, I slowly lower into the seat across from her. Each breath I take is slow and measured, keeping my pulse from thundering like a herd of wild horses.

Placing my folded hands in my lap, I remain silent, allowing her to speak first. The weight of her studying gaze scalds as I keep my eyes locked on the surface of the metal table. The tension between us becomes suffocating.

Finally, the servant returns. He sets a tray between us, breaking our eye contact when he leans forward. I can breathe again. Streaks of silver mix into the chestnut brown of his hair. Though his face appears young in contrast, the skin is bright and lacks any wrinkles, except for the deep frown lines on either side of his mouth.

After pouring two cups of dark tea, he removes the lid from a small dish, revealing an assortment of bite-sized shortbread cookies. When he stretches his arm out to set my cup in front of me, his sleeve shifts to reveal a mess of scars along his wrist. He pulls back quickly and tugs the material back into place.

In the center of each cookie is a dollop of thick, red jelly that looks like blood. It could be fruit preserves, but the warm copper tang that rises makes me doubt that. Once the servant finishes setting the table, he turns on his heel and strides out the door, leaving me alone with her.

Elizabeth picks up her cup and takes a dainty sip.

"Would you like a snack, Clara?" She motions to the small cookies.

"No thank you," I say, flattening my palms on the tops of my thighs.

The queen looks like any other young noblewoman, no older than I am. It's strange to think that Elizabeth has more power than anyone else in the world. She is responsible for every single vampire that has ever lived or ever will live.

"Drink," she says sweetly.

"I'm not—"

Her eyes narrow, flashing a crimson ring around the lavender irises. "I see Cassius has failed to do his job satisfactorily. He will force me to put him down at this rate," she mumbles against the porcelain cup as she takes another sip.

"What?" The word leaps from my tongue before I can stop myself.

Elizabeth sets her cup down and dabs the corner of her heart-shaped mouth with her napkin before looking at me. "Cassius did not tell you?" She quirks a perfectly shaped golden brow, her lip twitching into a sneer. "He was supposed to have trained you to behave."

She is threatening Cassius. I hold no love for the man, but I believe him when he says he is my ally. He might think he's safe from Elizabeth's wrath, but I don't doubt the lengths she would go to in order to punish me and keep Alaric on a tight leash.

"He is—he did…" I stutter. "I'm nervous."

That brings a smile to her face. "Nonsense." She waves a hand. "Relax, girl. I have come to deliver a gift to you."

My pulse kicks up, and I focus on calming it. "Why would you want to give me anything?"

"I have sent for our beloved crown prince. He should be here shortly."

Nerves prickle down my spine. I'm not sure what to say that wouldn't make things worse. I pick up my cup and take a sip, waiting for her to reveal more.

"Let's not mince words. My prince wishes to remain your master for the rest of your short life, and it's pathetically obvious that you have grown quite attached to him."

I sputter, nearly choking on the tea. Setting it back down, I wipe my mouth with the back of my hand.

"What would you do to have him back?" she asks. Her tone is almost bored.

I lean forward, unable to help myself, and whisper, "Anything."

Her face brightens, only adding to my curiosity. "Good," Elizabeth says, then claps her hands twice.

A moment later, the door opens. It's not Alaric but the manservant again. This time, he carries a small wooden box with intricate designs carved into it.

He presents the box to her on the table, taking away the tea and cookies to clear the surface. He bows to Elizabeth and then vanishes back out the door.

"I don't understand. Alaric's coronation, the oath binding… I thought…"

Elizabeth ignores me completely. Her long, thin fingers lift the lid. Lavender eyes gleam brightly.

Whatever is inside the box cannot be good.

Reaching in, she pulls out a small vial. Dark liquid sloshes inside the deep forest green glass with a cork.

"This is for you." Elizabeth holds it out to me. My mouth is suddenly dry, and I wish I had a bucket of tea to quench my nervous thirst. "Take it."

I reach out slowly, my hand trembling. If the queen notices, she doesn't let on.

"I know you think me cruel, and admittedly my past is colorful, but even I know compromises must be made for Alaric's sake. If I am to release him to you, I must know that you are deserving."

"Release him?" I ask dumbly.

She nods, offering a sweet smile. "I created him to be my prince. It is fated, but I am not so evil as to deny him what he wants." Elizabeth smooths her hands down her bodice. "You are human, and as such, will one day die from illness or age. After your death,

Alaric will take his rightful place. I waited for him for over one hundred and seventy years, a few more decades are nothing if it means his willing return. It is the least I can do for him… but I must know if you are worthy."

I examine the substance inside and realize it's not water. It's too thick and too dark.

"It's only blood," she says as if it's a small thing, and to a vampire, it may be.

But I'm human.

"Drink it," she says.

"Whose blood is it?"

Her lips purse, the joy leeching from her face.

"If I drink this—" I start.

"Then he is yours until the end of your natural life at which point, he will assume his rightful place at my side," she finishes.

Would I drink a small vial of blood to have Alaric back? He would do far more for me—he has done more.

If I could be sure Elizabeth's words were honest, I wouldn't hesitate. What she says sounds logical—give Alaric something he wants in exchange for his cooperation.

Does it matter? If she wants me to drink this and I refuse, then she will force it down my throat—and would most likely drown me with it in the process.

I pop the cork. The scent of cold metal rises up. Before I change my mind, I throw it back, trying to avoid the taste. I pray to the demons and saints that, for once, it *will* be this easy.

It goes down cold and syrup thick. The copper tang coats my tongue and throat. My stomach churns from the metallic taste that lingers, but that will go away soon.

She watches me expectantly. Perhaps she's waiting to see if I get sick and vomit on the floor so she can declare me unworthy of Alaric.

Heat builds in my veins, warm at first, but my blood grows hotter by the second until it feels like a thousand pins and needles stab my entire body all at once.

"What did you do to it?" I croak, clutching my throat in a useless attempt to stanch the pain. Each word is a hot knife slicing the inside of my throat.

Elizabeth tsks her disapproval, and instead of answering me, she leans back in her chair and folds her small hands in her lap.

The agony seeps into my muscles and bones until it feels as if some dark magic is flaying me alive, each layer of flesh being slowly carved away. My muscles contract until I can no longer control them of my own volition.

My spine arches with a snap. Each shattering

breath is filled with fire and acid. My chair tips, sending me crashing to the floor and curling into myself. The pain is unbearable, but it's more than that.

Something is very, very wrong.

I'm dying.

She poisoned me, and I took it without question. I was stupid for believing she would make this kind of a deal to gain Alaric's cooperation instead of using force or cruelty.

Writhing on the cold floor, I wait for death to take me, to end this excruciating agony I can't get away from.

A brush of fabric against my bare arm feels like burning ice. I peel my eyes open to find Elizabeth lying on the floor next to me, watching my suffering. Satisfaction sparkles in her eyes as her lips curl into a pleased smile. Elizabeth lifts herself up and brings her mouth close to my ear.

"You may bear his mark, girl, but he will never be yours," she says with a saccharine, sing-song lilt.

I cry out, clawing at my chest as pain lashes through me. The fire in my veins turns to ice. I can't even form words to respond to her.

This was all a trap—from the seamstress to Elizabeth's request for a chat and the offer of compromise.

Alaric strides through the door as if summoned from my thoughts, freezing as he takes in the scene, gaze shifting from me to Elizabeth.

Setting my focus only on him, I try to call out, but all I manage is a strangled groan.

With inhuman speed, he kneels at my side, gathering me into his arms. Every touch, every movement, is pure agony. Tears spill freely from my eyes, streaming down my cheeks in burning rivulets.

"Is she dying?" he asks.

Each inhale is like swallowing smoke. I can't stop breathing, but I wish I could. It's only making it worse.

Elizabeth remains silent and emotionless, leaving his question unanswered as well.

Alaric snarls, his fingers digging into my aching flesh of my arm and shoulder as he crushes me to him.

The light dims around the edges of my vision. I welcome it, willing myself to fall into the pit of darkness.

CHAPTER SEVEN

ALARIC

With each passing second, Clara fades away. I hold her to my chest. Her body spasms before going limp in my arms. Her chest flutters with weak, uneven breaths, but she is still alive.

Elizabeth's face is a stony mask, lacking all remorse.

I lay Clara gently back on the floor before rising and advancing as much as I dare. I might tower over her, but she holds more demon-sent power than anyone should ever wield.

"We had an agreement," I say, barely restraining myself from shouting at her. "What did you do?"

Elizabeth snarls, baring both sets of razor-sharp fangs, one upper and one lower. "I remember our deal, my *prince*," she spits the title like an insult. "I do not need you to remind me."

My back straightens, and I don't dare twitch a muscle or breathe for a long moment. Elizabeth's anger fades, and her eyes empty again.

"What did you do to her?" I ask barely above a whisper, attempting to keep control of myself.

She shrugs one shoulder.

Looking past her, my gaze snags on two teacups. Next to one is a small green vial. Speeding to the table, I pick up the discarded cork and bring it to my nose, inhaling deeply. The dark, smoky scent is strong. My hold loosens as realization dawns. It slips from my hand, but before it hits the floor, I snarl into Elizabeth's face.

"Demon blood? How much did you give her?" I grab her by the shoulders, barely retaining from shaking her.

I am rendered useless, my powers cannot oppose Elizabeth's, and any attempt to heal her would be in vain. The best I can hope for is that she only gave Clara enough to make her wish for death rather than a killing dose.

If the vial was even half full, her chances of surviving are slim at best. Humans are not built to withstand much power directly from a demon's veins, especially not the power of a demon already bonded.

Elizabeth's lavender eyes widen as she smiles demurely, not in the least bit cowed by my rage. "I had to know where your loyalty truly lies."

"I am doing as you order. You have always known that I will never love you. We made a deal—I would become your *consort*." I nearly choke on the word. "In exchange for Clara's life." My gaze falls on her deathly still form lying on the floor.

"Mmm," Elizabeth hums, circling me closely. She stops to my right, a thin finger taping the sharp line of her chin. "True… However, I cannot have you going behind my back to do demons only know what with this feral creature."

Elizabeth nudges her foot against Clara's leg to see if she still lives. A small, pained groan issues from her lips, flooding me with relief.

"I understood when you danced with her at the masquerade. It was to be expected once you did your duty by standing at my side for the first half. I even understood every other time you flocked to her —the mark can have that effect on those of us who are… *soft*." She whirls on me, her voice hardening to stone. "But to continue to do so when she has a new master is a blatant disrespect for me and our agreement."

She snaps her fingers. Two human servants enter, awaiting her command.

"Take her to the human quarters," she says without taking her eyes off me.

They grab her none too carefully, under her shoulders and knees, and carry Clara away. I open my mouth to object. Elizabeth's hand shoots out and grabs my hand, wrenching it toward her face.

Before I can process her intent, Elizabeth's mouth clamps down on my wrist. Her fangs pierce deep, the sharp points scraping against bone.

Her venom feels like acid burning through my veins. She pulls my blood in by gulps at a time. I tug on my arm, but her hold only tightens. Small beads of blood form along the tips of her fingernails. I fall to one knee before her, a cold sweat breaking out across my forehead.

Finally, she breaks away. Elizabeth grips my chin painfully, wrenching my neck back at a sharp angle until I am forced to meet her eyes. Crimson power engulfs the pale lavender irises, glowing brighter until I'm blinded to everything else.

"You will obey me, Alaric Devereaux. You will no longer betray me with your words or actions." Her voice vibrates with the command.

I struggle against it, but she has consumed my blood, taking in my power and infusing me with hers. My fingers clench at my side, arms shaking with the effort it takes to fight her.

"You will not go to that *human* again. You will search for me and stand by my side without question. You will be the perfect subject, the perfect prince."

My fist thumps against my chest, and my head lowers in a bow. Her power wends its way through my veins, digging its claws into every muscle.

No.

My will is surrounded by fog as thick as honey. The tension in every muscle relaxes, and the words that form on my lips feel strange and foreign. They are not mine, but hers.

"Yes, my queen."

CHAPTER EIGHT

CLARA

FIRE AND ICE SETTLE TO A STEADY ROAR IN MY EARS. The world sways sickeningly as my mind fights for a sliver of regained consciousness. I don't know which way is up, and every movement threatens to spill the contents of my stomach. I am going to be sick if it doesn't stop soon.

Voices whisper, coming from different directions.

Then… I'm falling.

I hit the ground with a cry out. No one responds as I writhe on the floor, dying. Fear trails its icy fingers over my skin. I can't control my body enough to speak or twitch a finger.

"Get out of the way," a man snarls.

His voice is familiar.

"Clara?" A hand pats my cheek firmly, sending wave after wave of stinging needles shooting along my face. "Clara, wake up. What in the Otherworld happened?"

His hand connects with my face harder this time. I manage a response, though it's nothing more than a groan of pain.

"Demon shit," Cassius mutters. His voice is louder now, closer. "Talk to me if you can."

I try to do as he asks, but the fire consuming me from the inside flares up again.

"What happened to her?" he demands loudly. "Who brought her here?"

Murmurs surround us, but a warning growl from Cassius silences them.

My consciousness swims with the shifting and swaying. I focus on Cassius's voice, trying to anchor myself to anything but the pain.

"Hold on, little bird," he whispers.

Wind rushes over us as he runs with dizzying speed. He shifts me in his arms. A door opens and closes. Then I'm placed on something soft and warm.

Two fingers pry at an eye, forcing it open. Blinding light fills my vision, and I collapse in on myself.

"Unholy demon shit, Clara, *your eyes.*"

The fact that he's this worried fills me with a deep sense of dread. I'm either dying, or something much worse is happening.

"My eyes?" I mumble.

He lets out a low growl. Cassius pries my eyes open over and over until I no longer scream in pain from the light and can keep them open on my own.

"No," I say, squinting through damp lashes to see I'm not in my room.

His brow furrows.

"Here." I flip my hand, only moving it slightly instead of shoving him away as I intended. "This isn't my room."

Hunching his shoulders, Cassius pinches the bridge of his nose. "Only you would fight me on the fact that I brought you to my rooms when you are half dead." He disappears and reappears in seconds, placing a damp cloth on my forehead. "We will talk if —*when* you get better."

Exhausted and weak from pain, I quit fighting, letting my body go limp.

Cassius cups my face with both hands. He closes his eyes for a moment, and when he looks at me again, they are filled with regret.

"I cannot heal you, little bird. Your eyes are solid black, and that can only mean one thing—a demon's power flows through you, and it's not Asmod's or

Cherno's. Our demon's powers cannot oppose another's. Was—"

I don't get a chance to hear the rest as darkness offers me a respite from the unbearable pain, and I sink into oblivion.

"He is lost to you," Varin's voice calls out to me in the dark.

I feel around blindly for something to tell me where I am and find nothing. The stale scent of damp straw wafts up as the demon moves closer, swirling up a soft draft of air.

"No, he's not," I bite out, fighting back a wave of sickening panic. I refuse to believe that—refuse to accept that… not after everything.

Varin sighs obnoxiously loud. "You are a stubborn fool," they say. "It would be better for you to let him go now, before things get worse."

I laugh sharply. "How could things possibly get any worse?"

Long, bonelike fingers trail down my arm. "Things can always get worse."

"I could die?" I offer a little too eagerly,

considering I am dying now. The reprieve from pain is welcome, no matter what it means.

"Take the ring, Clara. Let me help you. You cannot do this alone."

I want to argue, but I know they are right. Agreeing to a deal with a demon is not as straightforward as Varin would have me believe.

Taloned fingers wrap around my throat with a flash of red. The demon's face appears in the glow as their power rushes through me like an icy river, so cold it sears my nerves. In seconds, the light fades.

Varin grips my shoulders to hold me up, then whispers into my ear, "You have to wake up now."

I take a deep breath and open my eyes, frowning as I try to remember what happened. The musty air and mildew of the lower levels slowly fade.

Varin.

The harder I try to remember my encounter with the demon, the more it slips from my memory. It wouldn't be too hard to guess—in every conversation, the demon begs me to take the ring and bind myself to them.

I try to sit but find myself pinned down to the bed by an arm encircling my waist and a leg thrown over my mine. The warmth my half-asleep brain thought was a blanket turns out to be a vampire.

Demons and saints... Not again.

I pry Cassius's arm, but he clings to me in his sleep as if his life depends on it. "Shuuush," he mumbles sleepily, snuggling in closer. "Don't move yet."

Twisting within his death grip to face him, I plant my hands against his chest and push. My sore arms lack the strength to budge him. "Get off, you demon's ass or—"

One of his green eyes pops open as the sleepy grin falls away. "Do not talk." When I open my mouth to defy him, he presses his finger to my lips. "Clara," he says sternly. "You need to rest."

I wrinkle my nose, hating that he's right. I am exhausted. Waking up to his arms around my waist fills me with unease. I don't like how familiar he's become with me.

"The gold in your eyes is brighter in this light," he murmurs.

"Let me go," I hiss, ignoring his attempt at flirting.

Cassius doesn't move for several heartbeats. Then he releases his hold and is gone in a flash.

I breathe a sigh of relief and push myself up to sit against the headboard. That small exertion leaves me panting. My skin feels tender and raw. Everything just… hurts.

Asmod pokes their head out from under Cassius's pillow and eyes me. The thin silver tongue pokes out of their mouth, tasting the air. Slithering closer, they tap me with their smooth nose. I run a finger over their head and down the long body, over the smooth, dark green scales. The demon snake turns their head with a wink before slithering back under the pillow.

Cassius returns a moment later with a cup of water. He sits next to me and raises the glass to my mouth, helping me drink. The cool water hits my tongue and slides down my throat, easing the ache.

When I finish, he sits on the edge of the bed, bending a knee so he can face me.

A small bead of water slides from the rim of the cup down to his hand, unnoticed. "How do you feel?" he asks.

My first instinct is to brush him off. But the genuine worry in his eyes stops me, so I take a moment to scan my body from head to toe. "I'm sore… tired, but otherwise, I think I'm all right." I look away as I remember the past few days. Being nice doesn't make up for his deceit. "I would like to go to my room now."

"I will escort you."

I drop my legs off the edge of the bed and stand. My muscles are fatigued, but I think I can manage.

"I want to be alone." I clench my fists until my nails dig into my palms, then add, "You promised you wouldn't keep things from me anymore… but you still did."

Sighing, Cassius says, "I am sorry for not telling you about Alaric or the oath."

My chest tightens at the sincerity in his voice. The apology means more because he didn't offer excuses or explanations. Already I can feel the threads of anger and hurt begin to slowly unravel.

"Even though I'm furious with you, Cassius Wellington, I forgive you, provided this is the last time." I swallow. "But I need space before I can stop being angry."

His hand reaches for me, hovering for a moment before falling back to his side. "A promise now would be meaningless, so I will show you instead."

There is a small amount of comfort in hearing him acknowledge the damage his actions caused. I'm grateful he doesn't offer up another promise. He broke his word, and it hurt what little trust there was between us. Even still, my gut says he is still an ally.

For now, my focus needs to be figuring out what my next move will be.

Otherworld take me... I was a demons damned idiot to trust Elizabeth even for a second. But I doubt there was any choice other than drinking it willingly or by force.

Cassius nods. "It is midday. You will be safe."

He watches me walk away, no doubt looking for signs that I might pass out. I pause to glance back with my hand poised on the doorknob.

"I will be here if you need anything, Clara."

I nod once, then slip out the door, closing it quietly behind me. My pace is much slower than normal, and I'm nearly breathless by the time I get to the stairs. A light sheen of sweat has broken out across my forehead.

Turning the corner, I stop dead in my tracks as I look up. Alaric is halfway up the stairs heading toward his floor. I call to him through the connection we have with the mark, but he doesn't turn around.

Instinct takes over, and I follow him. Just as I reach the top, he closes the door to his room. I pause to catch my breath and then slip in after him. He flings his jacket on the back of the nearby couch, then turns to face me.

Alaric stands perfectly still. He shifts his weight to take a step, but his body jerks back. My gut twists as I approach him slowly.

"Alaric..." I say quietly. He doesn't respond. Dread

knots in my belly. There's something off about him. "We can't let the queen oath bind you—"

"You should leave," he says, voice flat and void of all emotion.

I take a step back, shocked by the unexpected reaction, not when he found me on the ground, nearly half dead last night.

His fingers stretch, then form tight fists. "Leave," he says again.

It makes sense for him to be cold and distant in public, but we are alone here. There's no evidence of anyone else around.

When I don't move, he strides forward and snarls viciously. I pull in a sharp breath. Gripping my upper arm with one hand, he opens the door with the other and leads me into the hall, releasing me. I stumble to catch my balance and turn just in time for the door to slam shut an inch from my face.

You trust him, I scold inwardly. *There is a reason for this.*

I seek him through the connection, calling to him, but he doesn't respond.

Varin's words leap to the front of my mind. *He is lost to you.*

What had Varin meant? Does it have to do with his strange behavior? I'd thought it a dream brought on by nearly dying...

I brace my hand against the wall and hurry toward the back stairs. I stop at the bust of the beautiful woman and push it off center. The familiar sound of stone grinding seems loud as the hidden passage opens.

Keeping a hand on the wall to guide me, I ignore the slimy feel of the damp stone and descend into the bowels of the castle.

I have to stop several times on the way down to the demon's cell. When I pull open the door, Varin doesn't even look up.

"You came to me in my head again last night," I say. It's not a question.

The stale scent of dust and mildew permeating this lower level assaults my nose. Varin inches closer, joints popping and snapping with every movement. The night-forged silver chains clank when they reach their limit, keeping the demon from reaching me. "You were close to death. You needed help."

"You-you," I stutter then swallow the hard lump of fear stuck in my throat. I force myself to ask the question, even though I dread the answer. "You said he was lost to me. Is he already oath bound to Elizabeth?"

The demon snarls, snapping their jaws, their large, sharp, charred teeth jut out of their lipless mouth. "He is lost to you, foolish girl."

I clutch at my chest. "I still feel our connection."

Varin tsks. "You should oath bind yourself to that other vampire because you will never get Alaric back."

"No! I can't accept that—I won't. There has to be some way…"

Varin extends their hand to me. "There *is* one way," they say slowly, unfurling their long fingers to reveal the ring.

"You are a horrible, deceitful thing. This was all your doing… your way of manipulating me into bargaining with you," I hiss, taking several steps back, regretting that I didn't stop to grab my dagger before coming here. "I will slay the queen before I free you!"

I turn to leave, but the door slams shut with a resounding clang. A long shadowy tendril of Varin's power retracts.

"That is a death mission, you foolish woman."

Half-hysterical laughter bubbles up. "I don't care."

"He has been compelled by the queen," they explain. "His mind is still his, but his body belongs to her. Soon, all of him will be under her control, and then there will be nothing in my power that can undo it."

Pulling in a breath, I hold it for a long moment. This is bad.

I take a tentative step forward. "But there *is* something that can be done?" I press.

Varin growls. The demon shrinks back into their shadowy corner. "Give him up."

"Never." I advance on the demon until my face is only inches from theirs. "I will do everything I can until there's nothing else, and time has run out."

CHAPTER NINE

CLARA

"You are a most difficult creature." Varin crawls forward in a way that makes their body look broken. Numerous joints bend at unnatural, painful angles as the demon sits back on their haunches.

"As are you," I retort. "Now let me out."

"Bargain with me."

"You forced me into this situation to make me think this is the only option left. I would rather deal with Elizabeth head on and die trying. At least I know her end game."

The demon stands on all fours, circling me. "I told you before that I need you alive."

"I am desperate, but I still know better than to make a deal with a scheming, deceitful demon."

Bending down, I snatch up one of their chains and

tug. Varin hisses and falls, rolling out of my way. I throw the door open, more than ready to put the miserable demon behind me once and for all.

"Wait!" they say, desperation in their voice. "I will help you." Varin reaches out a long arm, fingers stretching toward me, clawing at the air.

My hand tightens around the handle to prevent me from giving into the temptation. The power in their voice is too strong to ignore. "Don't bother. I won't take the ring or bind myself to you."

"Not a bargain."

"Then tell me your price," I demand. Listening to Varin's attempt to keep me here is a waste of time. We both know I have nothing of value to offer, and I have no intention of agreeing to what they really want.

"Your trust," they say simply.

"My trust?" I whirl on the demon.

Varin straightens, shifting deeper into the shadows. "If what I tell you saves your beloved, then you can decide if you will give me your trust of your own free will. If it doesn't, then you can slay me with your little dagger."

I hold out my hand. "Fine. Give me what I need to break the compulsion."

A chuckle. "What you need cannot be found within this dank little prison of mine."

I open my mouth to protest, stopping when they hold up a hand.

"The oracle witch knows a spell to break the queen's hold over him."

Irrational anger tries to rise to the surface, but I force it back down. The demon's reasons for withholding this information earlier are not important right now. Finding a way to save Alaric is the only thing that matters.

"Tell me where she is, and I will get it."

Varin motions for me to come closer. When I do, they point to the ground. I sit obediently. The faster I get the information, the sooner I can go and come back.

"Understand that this quest will not guarantee you success. But, if anyone can help you, it is her. However, be warned that even if you manage to make it there and back with the spell intact, there is still a chance it could kill him and his demon."

They could both die?

I shudder. That is not an outcome I want to think about, but Alaric has said he would rather die than be controlled.

Varin continues, giving me directions to the witch. I'm unfamiliar with the route, but I will find a map. According to the demon, the ride there should only take two days, one or two more with the oracle and two for the return trip. Even if it takes a little longer, I will be back in a week—less if I hurry.

I rise and dust myself off, glad that my strength is already returning because I will need it.

"Thank you," I say honestly as I move toward the door.

The demon stops me with a rattle of chains. "Wait."

I turn back to face them.

"Take the ring with you. I can help you." Each word out of the demon's mouth weaves a spell until their red eyes are the only thing I can see in this dark cell. I can feel skeletal fingers taking hold of my thoughts.

Stepping back, I pull in a long, deep breath and then release it, pushing the demon from my mind.

"No." I grit my teeth and uncurl my fingers.

Sitting in my palm is the silver ring, the same temperature as my skin. If it weighed any less, it would be unnoticeable. The shining band pulses with power, nearly vibrating with it, calling to me as Varin does. It gives me the feeling of being spoken to in the same hypnotic way the demon had moments ago. That power wasn't present in it the last time they slipped it into my hand.

Was it?

I don't know if that is their doing or that the band holds so much power it can barely be contained.

Turning my wrist, the ring slides from my palm. It chimes as it hits the stone and bounces.

"Try to manipulate me again, and I will never trust you even if this works." Then I step out of the cell and slam the door behind me. A plan is already taking shape.

Tomorrow night I will leave. That should give me sufficient time to rest and get everything I need together.

"Get up," Cassius's voice bites out.

I groan and roll away from him, pulling my blankets higher. "Tired," I mumble.

A hand strokes down my arm right before the blankets are ripped away. My eyes fly open as chilly morning air chases away any semblance of warmth.

I sit up and glare at him. "I didn't think we were training today. You said I needed to rest."

"You can't be that tired if it took you hours to get back to your room last night."

I must have been with Varin longer than I realized.

"I was feeling stronger from walking and wanted to test that..."

Twisting my fingers, I break off, hoping he can't see through my mumbling to the lie that it is. Cassius narrows his gaze while I stretch and make a show of nonchalance.

"I will be down in the training room soon," I say, running my fingers through my hair to work out the tangles.

Rather than leaving, Cassius takes a seat on the foot of the bed, resting an ankle over his knee and leaning back. "I will escort you. I need to evaluate how strong you are in order to avoid pushing you too hard."

Clearing my throat, I cross my arms under my chest, arching a brow when he doesn't move. Cassius mirrors the look, clearly not understanding my issue with his presence.

I twirl my finger. "Evaluate me all you like, but I'm sure you can restrain yourself until after I am dressed."

Cassius's eyes widen as he rises. Then he strides past me to stand at the door. His long, pale hair is pulled back with a thin leather tie at the nape of his neck and hangs neatly down the center of his back.

I dress quickly, well aware he is listening to see if I am winded by the simple task.

We stop by the kitchens to grab an apple that I devour before we reach the training room. The whole way there, I try to ignore the way he studies me like an animal in a cage.

I follow every order he gives, putting every bit of effort into executing each blocking technique he shows me until I master the smallest move. Today, I am the ideal human.

Crouching into position, I ready for the next attack. Cassius surprises me when he straightens and waves his hand.

"That is enough for today," he says. "You did well, I'm impressed your effort… It's so unlike you."

I shrug one shoulder, choosing to ignore how his eyes narrow on the last four words. Even I'm amazed to find I feel as good as usual. Maybe even better.

"You seem strong enough, but I don't want to take chances." Cassius eyes me. "We'll resume tomorrow."

I hold my breath, careful not to give away my excitement. This is the opportunity I need.

Once we finish putting the equipment away, I move toward the door, mentally ticking off the list of things I will need to gather before tonight.

Cassius's palm presses against the door, holding it shut. I turn to find him nearly pressed up against me.

"How are you feeling?" he asks. "You were poisoned with demon blood almost two nights ago."

Offering him my best grin, I say, "I promise I am fine. There's no need to worry."

He pulls me into a tight hug. "There's nothing wrong with being upset after what happened with Alaric," Cassius whispers, "I sent him away for your own good, I hope you can see that someday."

I wriggle out of his embrace and shake my head.

"Please don't fuss over me. I'm completely healed, and… Alaric won't be compelled forever." There's a twinge in my heart as I say his name.

He looks as if he wants to say more, but I don't want to waste the extra time he's unwittingly given me.

"I would like to go eat now," I say, ducking under his arm and hurrying through the door.

It's only a few hours' head start, but every minute counts.

Turning left down the hall, I walk as quickly as I can toward the kitchens. I need to secure enough food to sustain me for a week—some dried fruits and meats and plenty of teek bread. While dense and dry, the small cakes are compact and filling, making them perfect for long journeys.

I stand just outside the kitchen entrance, tapping my finger against my chin. *What can I tell the cook to keep her from being suspicious?*

"What could you possibly be up to now?" Della asks.

I whip around to find her leaning against the wall. "Nothing," I say, but the word is too sharp and too loud to be natural. "I'm getting something to eat."

Della straightens and circles in front of me, blocking the door to the kitchen. "Why do I not believe you?" She wrinkles her nose. "I don't know how anyone ever does. You're a terrible liar. Besides, I am fairly certain your meals are brought to your room." She pauses, her dark eyes dart around nervously. "Why are you roaming the halls without Cassius?"

"I told you. I need a few things." I lean to look past her as a servant exits the kitchen with a tray.

Della grabs my hand, holding on to it in a strangely friendly manner. "I know what happened... You shouldn't be outside your rooms alone like this... Wait." She drops my hand. "What *things* do you need from the kitchens?" she asks pointedly.

Demon shit. I said too much.

There's no way she'll stop digging until she knows everything. I chew on my bottom lip and debate what to do next. If I walk away now and go to my room, I'll waste all my extra time trying to ease her suspicions. But maybe she'll be willing to help, or at least keep quiet...

"Can I ask you for a favor?"

"A favor?" she repeats slowly.

"Yes, it's a thing friends do for each other sometimes."

Friends is a stretch, even by my standards, but I need to hurry.

Narrowing her eyes, Della steps forward and lowers her voice. "Out with it, or I will let Cassius know that you're acting strange… stranger than normal."

Her words sound cold, but if any other vampire catches me, both Cassius and I will have to answer to Elizabeth for my disobedience. I doubt either of us would make it out alive.

Then a thought strikes me. Could Della *actually* care?

"It's a small favor," I say.

She curls her fingers into her palm. "Stop procrastinating and tell me what you want."

I pull in a breath, then let it out, ready to tell her everything, but instead of the truth, what comes out is, "I haven't been eating as much as I should, and sometimes at night, I want a snack."

She sighs and grabs for me, but I step out of reach. "Clara, if you want a favor then you need to be honest, or I will drag you back to your room."

"You have to promise not to say anything."

"I knew you were up to something." She shakes her head, causing her smooth, black, shoulder-length hair to fan out. "But you know I can't do that."

My pulse drums in my veins. All hope of leaving tonight shatters. "Give me a day or two," I plead. "I only need a little time."

Della's eyes sparkle like two black diamonds. "Mmm, I suppose I *could* do that," she says after a painfully long moment.

I blow out a breath, shoulders sagging in relief. "I have to leave." I hold up a hand. "I'm coming back, but I need to find the oracle witch."

Della's mouth forms an O. She blinks twice, then grabs me by both arms and pulls me to the other side of the hall against a pillar.

"What?" she hisses. Her gaze darts rapidly up and down the hall to ensure no one is around to overhear.

"I need to find her so I can free Alaric from Elizabeth's compulsion," I explain.

She shakes her head. "How do you know he's compelled? It's possible he doesn't want you because you have Cassius's scent on you and you will be oath bond to him soon."

"It doesn't matter how—I'm going either way." I back up, ready to leave.

Della pales as she speeds to block my path, eyes

large and wild with an edge of panic. "All right," she says. "I'll help you."

I should question this sudden change of heart. Even if I don't understand it, she seems sincere.

In hurried whispers, I give her the list of food and other items I need. Then we agree to meet in my room in three hours. It's longer than I want to wait and will eat up almost all of my head start, but her help will prove invaluable.

I pace my room. It's a wonder I haven't worn a groove into the floor. The clock tower in the heart of Nightwich chimes, echoing through the castle. It's been five hours, and Della still isn't here. I can't leave without food or a map. Even I'm not foolish enough to think I'll find what I need out in the wild in the heart of winter.

When the door finally opens, I sag in relief.

Della tosses a pile of clothes onto the bed and holds up a bag with a strap. "I brought you a pack. The food is wrapped. It should last you six days if you ration it well. There will be rivers and snow to melt for water—"

"Did you find a map?" I cut her off.

Della reaches into the bag and pulls out a rolled piece of parchment.

I pluck it from her hand, then carefully unfold it. It's old and worn soft, though the ink is still dark. Tracing a line with my finger, I memorize the path from Nightwich to the forest on the far side of the Sunfall mountains. I could go around, but it could save half a day if I take the mountain pass.

"This is perfect!" Throwing my arms around her neck, I hug her.

She reaches up and pats my head before pealing me off. "Good, because I'm coming with you."

I blink, taking entirely too long to understand. "No," I finally manage to say. "Why would you want to come? I thought you were wanted to tell Cassius what I did."

Della straightens her shoulders and lifts her chin, giving her the appearance of a true lady. This reminds me how often I forget that the vampires I know—Alaric, Della, Cassius, and even Lawrence—are all leagues above me, even if they were human. I am nothing more than a poor girl from a small town, and yet, none of them has ever held it against me—at least not for long.

"I have my reasons," she says coolly.

"Then you can come."

I don't have time to argue. A vampire could come in handy out there.

She seems surprised when I agree so quickly.

Turning away, I hurry and stuff the clothes and things I'll need into the pack. A stray hair tickles the side of my face as I make sure my dagger is attached firmly to my arm.

Finally ready, I look to Della leaning up against the wall, but she won't meet my gaze.

Two strong hands land on my shoulders. My spine stiffens.

"Where do you think you are flying off to, little bird?" Cassius purrs in my ear.

CHAPTER TEN

CLARA

I spin coming face to face with Cassius, my heart leaping into my throat. Displeasure rolls off him in waves and every muscle in his body is taut. I can practically taste his barely restrained ire. I knew he'd be furious when he learned I left without permission, but I underestimated the extent of his anger.

I turn a glare on Della and hiss, "You promised not to say anything."

Her head snaps up, eyes flashing. "I said 'I suppose I *could* keep quiet.' I never said I would."

Throwing up my hands, I groan. *Vampires…*

"Please tell me you're not planning on doing anything stupid, Clara," Cassius warns with a low growl.

I drop my chin and sigh. "Think about it, Cassius,

the only things I *can* do are stupid. I'm alive only because Elizabeth is using me against Alaric. Otherwise, I would be dead or locked in the dungeon. If I was smart, I would obey her every word." My hands ball into fists, nails biting into the soft skin. "But that would mean standing by as Alaric is forced into his worst nightmare."

I take a step back, reaching for my bag. Defying him like this won't help his anger, but I have to do this. Alaric needs me, and I refuse to let anyone or anything stop me before I even get started.

"Where do you think you are going?" Cassius asks again, each word strained as if it's taking everything in him not to snap my neck.

"It doesn't matter. I'm going alone." I turn an icy glare on Della, directing the last three words at her.

Cassius grips my arm firmly, spinning me toward him, bringing his face within an inch of mine. "Are you insane? I'm not about to let you leave to go traipsing off to demons only know where on your own. You'll be killed in a matter of days, if not hours."

I open my mouth to argue and snap it shut because he's not finished.

"You forget that you are in *my* charge. What do you suppose would happen if anyone found out the human I'm supposed to train to behave—the human I'm supposed to oath bind to me—waltzed out of here without so much as a word? Do you care so little about the repercussions your actions have for others?" He looks at me expectantly.

Stunned by his outburst, I can only gape. He has lectured me, snarled, and growled, but I don't think he's ever yelled at me like he is now. I thought I knew his anger, but I was wrong.

My throat tightens with guilt.

"Well?" he asks when I don't answer.

I shake my head, struggling to find words. "Nothing… I don't know." My voice sounds hollow. "I didn't think…"

Cassius releases me suddenly and begins to pace.

"No, Clara, you didn't think. Because if Elizabeth found out you ran off on your own, she would send her guards after you—not to bring you back but to kill you, leaving your body where you fell for demons and wild beasts to feed on." He pauses in his pacing to rub his forehead.

Della groans from where she stands against the wall. "Ease off her. She sees your point."

"No," Cassius snaps, rounding on her. "She is my ward."

With each word spoken, time slips between my fingers. Desperation claws at my gut, my chest, my throat. He is right, but there is no other way…

"I'm going," I announce, nearly choking on the

overwhelming dread. The two vampires stop bickering to gawk at me. "Elizabeth can send her demons after me. This is the only way to break her compulsion over Alaric."

Cassius is before me in a flash, eyes pleading. "Clara…"

"Don't." I shake my head. Tears spring to my eyes, threatening to spill over. "He wouldn't allow me that fate. I can't let him suffer. No one deserves to be controlled like that."

Alaric's words replay in my mind, and it's all I can focus on. *I can feel my freedom slipping away every day. It's the one thing I've always feared.*

"How is it that you think you can break a compulsion spell? Where do you plan to go? What do you plan to do? Do you understand what it means to even attempt to break her hold?"

"He needs me, Cassius." I blink, and the first tear slides down my cheek—traitorous body. "I won't let him down. I'm going—with or without you."

Cassius's eyes darken. He reaches up and grabs the back of my head with one hand, pulling me forward and swiping my tears away with his sleeve. "Then I will go with you," he says quietly.

I scrunch up my nose.

"What? I thought you would be happy."

"You hate him." I'm grateful he won't stop me, but

I don't understand his willingness to help someone he considers a nemesis.

"Yes."

I wait for him to elaborate.

Finally, he says, "Do you really think so little of me? I may hate *him*, little bird, doesn't mean I want to see *you* die." He lifts my chin with a knuckle. "And since you won't give up this foolish mission, I might as well save myself a lengthy argument and accompany you."

Biting down on my lip, I reach for his hand and squeeze. "Thank you."

The corners of his lips twitch, and he nods. "Meet me at the stables in an hour." He strides toward the door and stops, turning to Della. "Stay with her."

"Where are you going?" I ask. "You don't even know my plan."

"I don't need to, little bird. If you're serious about this, then we'll need a reason to leave. I will provide that reason. I'll let Elizabeth know I have business to take care of back at the estate, and you can tell me your plans on the way."

He has a home outside this castle? Somehow that thought had never occurred to me.

Cassius takes my silence as his chance to leave.

I expected to make this journey alone.

Now I have two vampires for company. I don't know what to expect, but it will be interesting.

The night air is frigid, biting at the exposed skin of my face. I appreciate the warm set of fur-lined leather clothing and boots that Della thoughtfully collected for me, along with the list of supplies I'd given her.

Della leads the third horse from the stable. We haven't spoken more than five words to the other since Cassius left us alone.

Struggling to get my chestnut horse saddled and ready, I glance toward Della from the corner of my eye.

She focuses intently on preparing the other two. One is a pretty seal dun color, the other a dark bay.

I want to ask her the reason why she wants to come. It clearly has nothing to do with breaking Elizabeth's compulsion on Alaric. If I didn't know better, I would say Della is avoiding any conversation at all costs.

By the time I manage to saddle my mount, Della has the other two finished. Pushing my curiosity to the side, I pull out the map and study it while we wait for Cassius.

We can reach the forest by riding east, moving south past Gloamfarrow and around the foot of the Sunfall mountains, then north to the forest. It looks easy enough, but the pass will be faster and take us closer to where Varin said I will find the oracle.

"Is everything ready?" Cassius asks, removing a bag from his shoulder as he appears behind me with a soft whoosh of air.

I shiver, folding up the map, but before I can answer, Lawrence strides through the stable doors, dressed for a long ride and carrying a pack.

"Where is Asmod?" I ask, noticing the absence of the demon snake.

"Our demons will remain here at the castle," he says tightly.

Della comes to an abrupt halt next to me and lets out a low growl. The look of shock and mild betrayal twists her features. She turns to me, dark eyes pleading, as if she expects me to object. I raise a brow, not the least bit sympathetic to her plight. When she doesn't get her desired reaction, she turns a glower on Cassius. She mouths the words *you bastard* at him.

"Clara," Cassius says, ignoring Della's ire. "You'll ride with me." He strides past me to double check my —*our*—horse.

Lawrence looks displeased to be here. "Della insisted on going with you, though I cannot understand why. There is no love lost between her and Alaric," he grumbles.

"Then by all means, stay here. You don't need to come," she snaps. Her head pops up from the other side of her horse, leveling a glare at the man.

Lawrence's eyes widen at her sharp tone. "He is my friend. Not to mention the matter of how it would look when the woman I sired runs off with another man and Alaric's claimed human?" He tsks. "Don't insult me."

He mounts the dark bay horse with an effortless leap and turns his back toward her. Della's features crumple for a second before smoothing out. She lifts her chin, but there is still a wounded edge to her expression that tugs on my heart.

"It's fine," I say, not understanding what's happening between them. "If no one else is joining us, then we should go."

Della and Lawrence climb up on their mounts as Cassius reaches for my hand to pull me up. I look like a fish trying to walk on land compared to them as I scramble up in front of him.

"Why can't I have my own horse?" I grumble playfully, trying to hide my frayed nerves from the others.

Cassius snickers at my back.

I suppose this is for the best. My riding skills are minimal at the best of times, and his added body heat will be welcome once we reach the open plains. At least I don't have to worry about being thrown again. I shudder, remembering the pain of that night and the demon that nearly killed me.

"Which way?" Cassius asks.

"East."

He kicks the horse into a gallop, and the four of us ride into the night. We skirt the northern edge of Nightwich, and once we are away from the city, I tilt my head up and stare at the stars glinting across the endless, black sky.

When we are out in the open, Cassius leans in, pressing the corner of his mouth to my ear. "This will not stop Elizabeth from oath binding him."

I clench my teeth. "I know."

Alaric is living his worst nightmare, and this is only a solution for the smallest of the problems we face. I don't know how to prevent the coronation or anything else, but I will figure that out once he is no longer under her control.

Don't give up yet, Alaric. I will free you.

CHAPTER ELEVEN

CLARA

Della turns her head to glance back at the shrinking city behind us, her mouth pressed in a tight line, while I am drawn to the endless sky. I still can't get used to the silence of the night here. To be outside after sunset without the howl of demons and to gaze at the stars and remember my last night with Alaric...

"Now, little bird, tell me what we are doing," Cassius demands, breaking through my thoughts.

"We are going to the oracle witch. She has the power we need to break the queen's compulsion."

Cassius stiffens at my back. "No one knows how to find the oracle witch. She might as well be a legend."

"I do," I insist.

The arm around my waist tightens as he slows the horse to a trot.

"The oracle witch is a story. Even if she is still alive, she would have to be nearly six hundred years old. Witches don't live forever," Lawrence says, pulling his horse up alongside ours, "and even if she is, what makes you think she would deign to waste her magic helping a human?"

"She does exist, and she will give me what I need," I say.

"How can you be so sure?" When I ignore his question, he glances from me to Cassius.

"This is a fool's errand," Cassius says so quietly that I'm not sure he meant for me to hear over the pounding of hooves. "You should let him go."

My blood boils. I am sick of everyone telling me that. He would never give up on me, and I could never abandon him to a life he dreads.

"If any of you doubt me, now is the time to turn back, but I will not allow anyone to sabotage me."

"Do you even have a plan?" Lawrence asks.

Della scoffs from his other side. "Of course she has a plan. No human runs from Nightwich into the Sundown mountains without a plan in the middle of winter." The rising pitch of her voice doesn't lend confidence to her words. "You *do* have a plan, Clara. Tell them," she says almost desperately.

I chew on the inside of my cheek. I can't admit a demon set me on this mission. They would turn around in less than a heartbeat, and all three of them would make sure I didn't so much as *think* about stepping foot outside my room without one or more of them at my side.

"Once we find the witch, I will ask her for the spell to break the compulsion." It's a weak plan at best, but I have to assume Varin would have given me instructions if I needed to do more. After all, earning my trust rests on my success.

Cassius's hand squeezes my hip, and the leather of the reins groans under the force of the tightening hold in his other.

"What?" Della snaps before I can utter another word. "Did you at least think to bring payment in exchange for her help?"

Payment? That demon mentioned nothing about the cost. Panic rises as I do a mental inventory of everything I brought, and there is not a single coin among my possessions.

"Her magic will have a price," Cassius says gently.

I take a deep breath. "I will give the witch whatever she wants."

"You should be more careful about making such an offer, especially to someone so powerful they could ask for more than you're willing to give," he warns.

For Alaric, there is nothing I wouldn't give.

"It doesn't matter. She can rip my heart from my chest if that's what it takes."

Silence descends upon our little group. Lawrence, who has been silent for a while, gives me a sidelong glance, his expression, unreadable. When I meet his eye, he looks away.

I would offer the oracle witch my heart on a silver platter if she asked for it. I don't know when it happened or how, but something changed. It's impossible to pinpoint the exact moment it happened, but it was somewhere between my return to Windbury and agreeing to come to Nightwich with Alaric.

Somehow, that vampire, my mortal enemy, became dear to me. I regret not telling him as much the last time we were together. With the steady swaying of the horses, I lose myself in thoughts and memories.

We ride until dawn in silence, slowing to a walk halfway through the long night. Eventually, the sun lightens the sky on the other side of the mountains, bringing a small amount of warmth with it.

Cassius pulls the horse to a stop, and Della and Lawrence follow suit.

"We'll rest here for a few hours," Cassius says as he dismounts.

I try to move my leg over the horse's neck, but two strong hands grip my waist and lift me off the horse, setting me on firm ground. Taking one step, I stumble, not expecting my legs to be so sore and tired. Cassius steadies me.

Lifting my head to thank him, I swallow the words down. He's not even looking at me, too busy having a silent conversation with Lawrence. Cassius nods decisively. Then Lawrence and Della take off running on foot toward the south with vampire speed.

"Where are they going?" I ask.

Cassius drags his gaze to mine, letting go of my arms when he's sure I won't fall over. "They are headed south to Gloamfarrow for supplies. You should have a seat. You look exhausted. Did you sleep at all?"

"Was I supposed to sleep?"

He doesn't answer, only laughs, pulling out a small packet from my bag and handing it to me. Unwrapping the wax paper, I break the teek bread in half and offer it to him. He waves it off.

"That will not sustain me," he says with tension in his words that makes me nervous. "Sit and eat. I will gather wood to build a fire."

I look at the vast openness of the world around us. "You need to feed."

Should I offer him my blood? Afterall, it's my fault that he's out here. With how fast he secured our reason for leaving and packing a small bag, I doubt he had the opportunity to feed before we left Nightwich. He either didn't trust me to wait for him, or he understood the urgency... I suspect that it's the former—he practically said as much.

Cassius eyes me like he might want to do more than feed. I take a large bite of the teek bread and take in the vast plains. The ground is hard and flat. So far, other than a handful of copses and stretches of dried grass, the earth has been mostly hard, cracked mud.

At my back is the edge of a small, wooded area. The sound of a nearby stream follows the line of trees.

"Do not worry yourself about that, little bird. Della and Lawrence will bring reserves. We planned for this. Now sit and eat."

I shake my head. "I'm not going to stand around and watch you do all the work. Let me help."

"Fine, you can help me gather what we need. Look for dried moss, leaves, and sticks. I'll gather the pieces."

We go our separate ways, gathering everything until there is enough for Cassius to build a fire that will last several hours. He kneels, arranging the wood we gathered, then pulls a flint from his pocket and strikes again and again. Sparks fly, landing on a nest of moss and twigs nestled in the center.

"Why don't you take the horses to the stream for water?" He braces his hands on his knees and straightens, then points toward the trees. "It will give you a chance to stretch your legs while I set up the tent."

Taking up the horses' reins, I lead them to the nearby small stream surrounded by a small copse of barren trees. The trunks are a ghostly white with dark patches that look like claw marks. I munch on the teek bread, struggling to chew. Even taking sips between bites, it takes a while.

I wrap my cloak tighter around myself. It's cold, but at least we don't have to deal with snow or wind. I pat the horses as they drink their fill then tie their leads to a low-hanging branch so they can eat the dry grasses as we rest.

A small leafy bush with thick, dark berries catches my eye. We had several behind the house in Littlemire. Kathrine used to call them night berries because when they are ripe, the red is so dark it's nearly black.

My mouth waters, remembering the things mother used to make with them. She would send

Kitty and me with bowls to pluck as many as we could. Then she would spend the day making pies and jams. I tried helping once, and ended up making a mess of things, dropping half a dozen eggs on the floor.

I squat near the bush and pluck a handful, popping one berry in my mouth at a time. It's juicy and sweet. Perfect. Certainly more appetizing than the teek bread alone. I alternate between bites of bread and a few berries. When I finally finish the bread, I guide the horses back to camp.

Cassius waits for me in front of the fire, staring into the flames. Wordlessly, I take a seat next to him. I remove my gloves with my teeth, then rub my hands together, soaking up the heat. When my fingers finally thaw, I reach inside my pocket and pull out the map, spreading it flat on the ground to study it in detail.

"We will go around the foothills and enter the forest from the south," Cassius says.

My head whips up. He gazes straight ahead into the distance.

"No. That will take time we can't spare. We go through the mountain pass."

Cassius looks at me as though I've sprouted a second head. "No way in the Otherworld. Clara, I know you're worried about time, but we don't know what the pass holds. It's uncharted. We can't take that risk."

"Where else would it lead?"

"To a wall of rock or perhaps a sharp drop off into a ravine. There are countless paths that lead nowhere, it is a labyrinth inside there. No one who has ever ventured in were ever heard from again."

I stand, folding the map and shoving it back into my pocket.

"You are being reckless, Clara." His words are sharp. He rises and steps in close, waving his arms out to the side. "Everything about this is—"

"I know!" I shout, clenching my hands into fists. Then softer, I repeat, "I know."

"Then use your head."

My cheeks sting from a mixture of frustration and cold. "It may not seem like it, but I am trying. I have to do this, but..." I swallow the lump in my throat. "What chance do I have of making it, if you all doubt me at every turn?"

Cassius presses his fingers to his temples and rubs small circles, muttering under his breath. "You are right. I don't know what's going on in your head, but I trust you," he says. He holds his palm up to keep me from interrupting. "But I need you to be honest, and tell me everything."

Everything. He wants me to tell him how I learned

about the oracle and how I know exactly where to find her.

But that would mean admitting everything about Varin, which I won't do. Lying to him doesn't feel like the right option either.

I avert my eyes, focusing on a spindly-looking plant with wispy leaves. "I can't do that."

"Clara…"

"I can't tell you everything, so please don't ask." I shake my head. "But I will tell you what I can."

He steps in closer and smooths a hand over my head and down the length of my hair. "What have you gotten yourself into?"

I try to smile but can only manage a rueful uptick of one corner of my mouth.

"Will you compromise to go around now, and if we see a way through from within the forest, we will take the pass on our return?" he asks.

I press my mouth into a tight line and think about it. He's right. If the way in is like a maze, then it could cost us more time.

"Yes," I say.

"You should rest now, little bird," Cassius says.

I reach out, resting a hand on his forearm, and wait for him to meet my gaze. "I'm sorry."

His brows crash together in confusion. "You have nothing to apologize for."

"Yes, I do. I would have left without stopping to think what consequences you would have suffered for my actions until it was too late." My fingers tighten. "I would have cared, Cassius…. I *do* care."

His face softens with a small smile. He nods, then jerks his head toward the tent. "Go now, little bird. Rest while you can."

Rising up, I walk toward the thin canvas tent, and stop outside to look over my shoulder. "I'm glad you came, and thankful that you're helping me keep a level head."

Without waiting for a reply, I climb inside and lay on my back staring at the dark material that covers me like a starless sky. Listening to the soft snapping and crackling of the fire I try to sleep, but my nerves are wound so tight that even exhausted, I find it impossible.

The sky gradually grows darker.

I sit up when I hear voices outside the tent. The others must have returned. Unable to hear what they are saying, I crawl forward and lift the flap. Lawrence holds out a pack for Cassius. He catches my eye, and I shrink back inside.

Sitting back on my haunches, I wait. Footsteps crunch on dried grass. A cold gust of air sweeps in as the flap is pulled wide. I shiver.

Cassius crouches at the entrance. "It is time to go." He takes me in. "You didn't sleep at all, did you?"

I shake my head then take his outstretched hand.

We are riding again before the sun is fully set, skirting tightly around the foothills of the Sunfall mountains. I breathe a sigh of relief as the top of the forest comes into view along the edge of the horizon.

"There are stories and legends about what lurks in these forests," Cassius murmurs into my ear. "The creatures that are said to inhabit them rival demons. Some say that the local fauna mated with ancient demons and became twisted things that are made of magic and tricks."

I snort. "That's nothing more than a children's story."

"Are you sure about that, little bird?"

Twisting in the saddle, I swat playfully at his arm. "I'm not a child so you can stop trying to scare me."

He chuckles, and I face forward again, gaze rolling skyward with a smile.

After a while, I'm too tired to stay awake much longer. My eyes are heavy, and with each blink, it's a fight to open them again. Despite the warm furred clothes and Cassius's body heat at my back, the chill of the night creeps into my bones.

I brush a hand along my dagger strapped to my

thigh. My thoughts drift to Alaric, wishing he was with me.

The blood in my veins feels sluggish, as if slowly solidifying to rivers of ice. My teeth chatter. I tug the edges of the cloak tighter, pressing back into Cassius and attempt to soak up his warmth.

"Clara?" Cassius says my name, but his voice is muffled.

I sway in the saddle.

Turning my head, I open my mouth to answer. The world shifts with me and doesn't stop. Icy air rushes past my face as my limbs refuse to cooperate. Cassius reaches out to me from atop the horse.

I land with a hard thud. My head smacks against the ground, and stars explode across my vision.

CHAPTER TWELVE

CLARA

I try to move, but I can't feel my body. The dull throb in my head is the only thing telling me that I'm still alive. The world is nothing more than dark shapes moving against even darker shadows. Faraway voices call my name.

"What's wrong with her?" Lawrence demands.

My stomach aches with a stinging heat, growing unbearable as it spreads like burning oil through my veins. I try to keep from moving to stop the spinning in my head.

"She's ice cold," Cassius's deep, rich voice says near my head.

"Stupid girl. She should have said something," Della mumbles, though her words lack their usual sharp edge. "We never should have allowed her to go on this foolish mission."

Everything hurts. The muscles in my back contract, arching my spine sharply. Then my body seizes.

Strong hands grip my shoulder and hip, rolling me to the side just as I retch, emptying the contents of my stomach onto the ground.

Once the tremors finally cease, I sag.

Arms encircle me, holding me tightly to a warm body. Cassius's scent surrounds me as his ear brushes my mouth.

"Clara?" Then louder, he says, "Demon shit, she's not breathing."

Still too weak to open my eyes, I want to tell him I'm fine, I'm only exhausted, but my mouth refuses to form the words.

He leans in again and inhales deeply.

Did he... sniff me? *When I wake up, I'll have to speak to him about his inappropriate behavior.*

The three vampires talk, but they speak too fast for me to understand anything they say. The heaviness of deep sleep calls for me, but I fight it, wanting to know why Cassius is upset.

The world shifts and rocks.

"Clara?" Cassius's voice is close again. "Did you eat or touch anything?" He shifts me again and sets me down on something soft. "Clara… *Clara,* talk to me," he growls.

Two palms press down on my chest. Red light flares, blinding even through closed eyes. A deep, resounding ache infiltrates my body, wrapping around the sharp, stabbing pain.

I want to push his hands away. Power forces its way through my body in waves of crimson, again and again.

My lungs expand painfully as I draw a deep breath. The cold air burns my throat, chased by a deep ache that settles over me like a blanket.

Demons take me, I *wasn't* breathing.

"Clara, what did you touch or eat?" he asks again.

"Wild berries," I mumble.

Cassius grabs my wrist and yanks my glove off. My fingers brush against his face as he inhales. *He really needs to stop sniffing me.* Then his hand tightens around mine.

"Demon shit. Those weren't wild berries, Clara, those were Cacodemon berries, they're poisonous."

It isn't until he utters those words that I understand, though I don't get a chance to think about it as nothingness swallows me up.

With a gasp, I sit up, clutching at my chest. My lungs burn. I blink into the darkness and try to remember where I am. It's too warm for winter.

The last thing I remember was riding toward the mountains with no shelter for as far as the eye could see. The ground beneath my palm is flat and smooth.

Am I in a cell?

Footsteps over stone approach. Scrambling to my feet, I ready myself. I reach for the dagger on my thigh, but it's not there.

Demon shit, where did it go?

A figure takes shape from the shadows, gradually becoming clearer. The approaching man is tall and familiar. As if a veil is lifted between one step and the next, Alaric's features become crystal clear.

This has to be a hallucination. We are miles apart, and he's under Elizabeth's control.

The way he looks at me cracks my heart with that painfully beautiful smile on his lips. It is the same expression from a few nights ago.

"Alaric…" I run toward him, stopping only an inch away. I want to hold him, touch him, but I'm afraid he will dissipate into smoke and mist.

He frowns, tilting his head. "My dear Clara, what are you doing here?"

"Where are we?" I ask.

He reaches for my hand and takes it in his. It's solid and warm, and he feels... *real*. "You shouldn't be here."

Alaric's worried, but I can't help but be in awe of this moment. Tears prickle the backs of my eyes.

"Is it really you?"

He smiles sadly. Even though there doesn't seem to be a source of light, I can see him perfectly. Alaric brings our hands up to my eye level, palms pressed together as if we'll dance, then entwines his fingers with mine. I can't stop staring at him.

"I don't know if this is real... but if it is, I want you to know that I will save you, Alaric. I promise I will," I swear in a tumble of rushed words.

His midnight eyes darken. "Save me? My dear Clara, I am afraid that is impossible. Stab me through the heart if you want, but do not allow me to hope because that is a torture I cannot endure."

I run my fingers across his brow and trace along the features of his face. There are so many things I want to ask and say, but in the end, I say, "Don't give in just yet. Wait for me."

"I am a prisoner. My body and actions are no longer mine," he nearly growls the words. His fury and frustration shine through, lighting his eyes with a glowing red ring. "I will never be free unless Elizabeth releases me from her power, and she will never do that."

Wrapping my arms around Alaric's neck, I pull him into a tight embrace.

"Give up on me, Clara."

"Would *you* give up on *me* if I were in your place?" I demand, leaning back to glare at him for saying something so absurd.

"You are in my blood and in my bones… in my very essence. I could never give you up, my dear Clara," he says sorrowfully.

"Then don't be so foolish as to ask that of me."

He cups my face and pulls me in, placing a kiss on my forehead. "I know you will do everything you can —demons help anyone who gets in your way—but I would not blame you if you went no further. You owe me nothing."

Pressure from the building tears turns into painful throbbing at my temples. Does he think I'm doing this because of my debt to him?

"It's not about owing…" I thump my fist weakly against his chest. "You're an idiot, Alaric Devereaux."

He chuckles at that, tugging on my hand, so I step into him, and his arms encircle me.

I bury my face against his chest. Demons and

saints, he feels exactly as I remember. I don't know if this is a side effect of the cacodemon berries or if some other magic is coming into play. Either way, I am thankful for this moment.

"Keep fighting… keep fighting her hold," I whisper.

"I don't know if I can."

I sniffle as the first tear falls, then another, until my vision clears. "You can. You have to."

He says nothing.

A feeling of fullness swells in my chest, so close to overflowing. There is a desperate need to say something, but I'm unable to find the words. I rise up on my toes and grab Alaric's collar to pull him down into a kiss. Hallucination or not, this is real.

Alaric pulls away before I'm ready and rests his forehead against mine. His eyes remain closed as he whispers, "My dear Clara, you will shatter me before this is through."

"I—"

The sweet smile slips from his mouth. His glittering eyes dull, becoming unfocused. I almost don't recognize him as the queen's control over him tightens. Alaric's face contorts as he resists.

"*Go*," he growls.

His hand reaches forward. Fingers slide through my flesh, then wrap around my heart and squeeze.

My mouth opens to ask what he's doing, but all I can manage is a gasp.

I expect rivers of blood to pour down my front with his hand buried deep in my chest. But there isn't a single drop.

Red light flares, blinding me, then the demonic power fades to black.

I pull in a deep gulp of air as my eyes fly open. My insides feel as though they were removed and put back by some cruel demon. Warm hands grab my face as I flail, gasping.

Cassius's face is within an inch of mine. Red light sizzles off his fingertips. Beyond him, I see the dark material of the makeshift tent. The gentle crackling fire outside is soothing amid the heartache. Della and Lawrence's voices drift into the covered space. They're bickering—again. But strangely, even that sound is welcome right now.

"Your heart stopped for a moment," Cassius explains, holding me against him. He kisses the top of my head and rocks gently. "You had me worried, little bird."

Tears spring to my eyes again, and I don't even try to fight them. Alaric feels farther away than ever. Remembering his words makes my heart ache. How can he think I would ever give up on him?

I will never give up.

Whatever it takes, I won't stop until he's free of Elizabeth.

Cassius runs his hand up and down my spine in soothing strokes until my tears run dry.

When I manage to compose myself, I am determined more than ever to get to the witch.

"Where are we?" I ask, each word feeling like it has to claw its way out of my already raw throat.

"We're a few hours south of the forest to the east of the Sunfall mountains."

Then we're close. I drop a hand and brace myself against his knee. When I try to push up, Cassius shifts his leg, taking my support out from under me, and holds me tighter.

"Let me go." I wriggle uselessly.

"You need to rest, Clara," he says.

"I can rest later."

His fingers dig in as he lowers his voice. "First, you stop breathing, then your heart… It's only been a few hours. You can't keep pushing yourself without allowing your body to recover."

I press a hand to my chest and feel my heart

beating. For nearly dying, it seems strong. "It's beating now. I promise I won't eat anything else unless it comes from my pack," I say mulishly.

Cassius growls and releases me. I fall from his lap to the ground and roll to my stomach. Lifting my head, I look up into his annoyed face. Red encircles his green eyes. Neither of us moves or blinks as if this was a test of willpower.

"You need to understand the gravity of what happened. If you were not marked, you would have been dead within minutes of eating those berries. It is the reason you hung on long enough for me to aid in your healing." Gradually, his expression softens, and he heaves a weary sigh. "Rest for me… and if not for me, then for Alaric," he bites out the name. "He would want you to recover fully before continuing on."

Pushing myself up to sit across from him, I glare, hating that he used Alaric against me. I take a calming breath, then exhale through my nose. "Fine," I say eventually.

"Thank you," he says, moving to let me lay down. "Even vampires can't stay awake indefinitely."

"Where are you going to sleep?" It hasn't escaped my notice that there is only one place set up in this tent, and it's too small for the both of us.

He gestures to the dirt floor and then lies down on his back, clasping his hands over his stomach. I instantly feel bad. Sharing a cramped sleeping space isn't ideal, but he's also not a dog and deserves better.

I poke his cheek. Cassius opens one eye and raises a pale brow in question.

"Move." I sigh. "You don't need to sleep in the dirt."

The corner of his mouth twitches in a half-smile. I watch him sit up. His movements are strangely sluggish and human, as if he has lost the weightlessness of his immortal strength. We resituate the blankets, then lay side by side.

I curl up on my side, using my arm as a pillow, and study his profile. "You really are tired."

Cassius lists his head to the side and looks at me. "Yes. There is strong magic nearby dampening our powers. We'll be weaker until we get used to it." He straightens his head and closes his eyes again. "Get some rest now, little bird. What's coming will not be easy."

CHAPTER THIRTEEN

CLARA

"You are much stronger than could be expected after the reaction you had," Cassius says as we ride several lengths ahead of the others. His words are quiet and partially stolen by the wind.

I glance over my shoulder. "Mmm?"

Cassius presses his mouth to my ear and says, "I have watched you recover from poison twice in a matter of days. How you survived even once is beyond me. First demon blood then cacodemon berries. Even marked, you are still human. If I didn't know better, I would say you were bound to a demon."

Swallowing thickly, I reach up and pull the collar of my cloak higher to partially hide my face, afraid I will give something away.

"Well, I'm not, or I'd be a vampire, wouldn't I?" I return my gaze to the forest ahead and focus on the beat of hooves over the winter-hardened ground. There's no way the exchange of information with Varin could have bound us in any way. They are not my demon.

The first time Varin came to me, they said being touched by a third demon's power made me malleable, and others would only increase that.

How many demons have touched me with their power?

Alaric used Cherno to compel and heal me. The second was the demon that clawed my leg when I tried to run away from Alaric, and the third when I returned after Kitty's wedding. Victor both compelled me and sent his demon to possess and haunt me at night.

Mother and Varin each healed me after one of Kerin's attacks. During the reclaiming, both vampire "suitors" compelled me. And then Cassius used Asmod's power to heal me a handful of times. I have been touched by the power of nine demons, four directly and five through their vampire masters.

Could that have given me the strength to bear the power of demon blood? Perhaps Elizabeth was careful to keep the amount just shy of a lethal dose.

Though it's just as likely that it was nothing more than pure luck.

As for the berries… I would be dead if it weren't for Cassius and the rapid healing ability I've gained through Alaric's mark.

"You have a point," Cassius murmurs in agreement, bringing me back to the present.

"Perhaps you are more adept at healing than you realize."

"Well," he says. "Either way, I failed to warn you about potential dangers in this area. Wild berries don't grow near the mountains, only cacodemon berries. They look, smell, and taste the same, but they are deadly. Untapped power leaks from out of the Otherworld in this region and without enough demons to temper it, the local plants and wildlife become infected. There is truth behind every children story."

I appreciate the explanation and how he doesn't make me feel stupid for my mistake.

Silence yawns out between us. I push thoughts of demons and their power aside to contemplate the man at my back.

Nearly every word from his mouth is harsh and cutting or in some way deceptive. He keeps secrets and breaks promises as it suits him.

I didn't believe him when he first claimed to be my

friend. When we met, he saw me as a possession to take from Alaric. But as we spend more time together, I continue to discover more facets of who he really is.

After I recovered from the demon blood, Cassius has shown himself to be a better man than I have given him credit for, starting with his apology.

Cassius could have stopped me or insisted we return to Nightwich after I ate the berries. But instead, he's helping me save a man he claims to hate. He has given me his full support and saved my life.

He's doing this because he truly is my friend.

Halfway through our trek for the day, we break for lunch near a spring. I pace back and forth to work the ache out of my muscles from being on a horse for so long.

I chew unenthusiastically on my meal of teek bread, already tired of the bland taste. At this point, a branch might be more appetizing. It would undoubtedly be less dry.

Cassius pulls a waterskin from our saddlebag and takes a short drink. When he's done, he passes it to Lawrence and then to Della. Judging from how little they consume, they are rationing their blood stores.

I wrap the remaining chunk of teek and slide it into my pocket. Leading the horses to the spring, I let them drink their fill and eat what grass they can find. The steady burble of water is relaxing.

"Are you ready to go?" Cassius asks from behind.

Letting out a squeak, I round on him. On instinct, I arch my arm across my body, swatting his hand away.

"Demon shit, you startled me," I hiss, pressing a hand to my chest to keep my heart from jumping out of my skin.

He smiles satisfactorily, all fangs, though it makes him appear more endearing than vicious.

Has my life changed so much that vampires look more affable to me than the dangerous and powerful creatures they are? Or have I been blessed by the saints of the Otherworld to find several good people who happen to be vampires?

Taking up the reins, I start walking with the horses. I don't get far before Cassius falls into step beside me as if we are strolling through a garden.

"I never thanked you for taking care of me after what happened with Elizabeth."

"I was glad to and would do it a thousand times over," he says casually.

Heat stings my face despite the cold air. "Why?"

Cassius takes my arm, stopping me. I force myself to meet his gaze. "I have already told you why."

My brows crash together. *When had he told me?*

"I care for you," he adds.

Those four simple words form hallow a pit in my stomach. They are vague enough to hold more than one meaning. "Why?"

He takes the leads from me as we make our way back toward camp. I swallow, clasping my hands together to stop from fidgeting.

"Simple," he says with a half-laugh. "You are reckless, spiteful, sharp with your words, impulsive, rude... You are the farthest thing from a lady! Demons and saints, you're practically feral." He laughs as he lists nothing but negative traits, ticking each attribute off on his fingers.

I level him with a glare.

The humor fades from his expression, darkening his eyes as his mouth tugs down at the corners. "And you have the wicked heart of a vampire in you, but most importantly, little bird, I admire how you will go to the ends of the earth for those you care about. I should be so lucky to one day find myself on the receiving end of that trait as I have all your others." He lowers his voice even further and adds, "These are no doubt the very qualities that captured the heart of our dear prince."

I don't know how to respond to that, so I say nothing.

We approach the others. Both Della and Lawrence avoid my eyes as they mount their horses. Without a word, they urge the beasts into a trot, giving us space. My face warms wondering if they overheard our conversation.

Cassius leaps up onto our horse and extends his hand out to me. I take it, letting him lift me into the saddle.

"You've been more of a friend to me than I thought possible. I didn't trust you—at first I thought it was a trick, but I don't..." I trail off as he urges the horse to move into a steady gallop.

Cassius grins broadly. "The only thing I ask of you is your friendship. If I have that, then I know my life is safe in your hands."

"Then you have it." I might be half mad to offer, but he has proven himself in a short time—even if he does give me too much credit. I am only human and lack any power that comes close to that of a vampire. Of all Elizabeth's creations, Cassius is second only to Alaric.

"Why are you doing this?" he asks abruptly.

"Doing what?"

Cassius gives me a disapproving look, then juts his chin out toward the forest.

"He loves me," I say as if it's an answer.

I owe him. Alaric has done everything for me. He is the best friend I've ever had and better than I deserve. I can't leave him to the one fate he dreads.

"And you love him," Cassius says, then adds, "Most people will never get the chance to see if their love is real enough that they would risk everything for it."

His words strike me like a punch to the chest.

Demon shit.

Beyond the doubts and uncertainty, the truth was always there, hidden by a veil of fear. Fear that the mark would manipulate our friendship into something that was not real.

But I loved him even when I thought he would never feel the same.

When I saw him with the queen, and they looked like lovers, I still wanted to be with him, no matter the cost, because it would hurt more to leave.

Whether our feelings were forged by the mark or existed before—*it is real.*

My throat works to swallow my heart back down.

With or without the mark, I love him.

I love Alaric.

It's why I went to a demon for help and why I will

never stop trying to save him from the waking nightmare Elizabeth has trapped him in.

I hold my breath and nod because I can't allow myself to confess aloud to anyone else when I haven't even said the words to Alaric.

"Did you tell him?" Cassius asks tentatively.

My heart squeezes. Before Alaric stepped into my life, I never knew what it meant to have someone care about me for who I am, not because they find me useful or convenient.

Of everyone in this world, it was a vampire who loved me first.

"No." I look away in shame, then say, "He deserves to know…"

"You will get your chance." Cassius slides his arm around my shoulders and hugs me. "But I still care for you, little bird."

My spine stiffens. I feel soft laughter against my back rather than hear it. "Cassius—"

"I will not come between you, but just how you cannot change your feelings, I cannot change mine."

After that, silence settles like a heavy weight between us. Chewing on the remaining teek bread, I take in the details of the forest as we approach.

Breaking off another bite I glance toward Della. Her face seems thinner than yesterday. It hasn't escaped my notice that they have yet to consume more than a small amount of blood since we left. What Della and Lawrence managed to bring from town is already running low. I doubt they have enough to make it any farther than the oracle witch.

I have no idea what we'll do for the journey home, especially if we take the mountain pass. How long can a vampire last without fresh blood? Will I need to feed all three of them? I suppose we will cross that bridge once we come to it.

CHAPTER FOURTEEN

CLARA

The forest's edge looms ahead. We will be there in about an hour. Grass springs up from the ground, dry and brown from the winter. The closer we get, the more sporadic patches of green blades appear until the lively color takes over. It should be long dead, but the trees are full as if it was the height of spring rolling into summer.

The horse's rocking gait lulls me into relaxation. I lean back against Cassius, his arm bands around my waist. My eyes slide closed as I mentally run through the plan over and over.

Find the oracle. Get the spell. Return to Nightwich. Break Elizabeth's hold over Alaric.

There is a lot to figure out after that, but at least Alaric will be there with me to help.

The horse lurches to the side with a loud whinny, tossing its head. My eyes fly open from the sudden jerk. Cassius's arm tightens as he steadies the mount with his free hand.

He turns the horse's head to face the opposite direction, then leaps to the ground sweeping me along with him. My pulse is still hammering loudly in my ears as the others dismount their spooked horses as well.

"What happened?" I ask breathlessly, turning in a half circle to scan the trees and surrounding area. But find nothing that might scare a horse.

"The power here is too strong," he says matter-of-factly.

The vampires remove the bags from the horses and drop them on the ground, then begin removing the tack and brushing them down.

Cassius slaps our horse on the rump. It takes off at a full run as if its life depends on getting away from us. Seconds later, the other two horses follow after it.

"What are you doing? The witch is in the heart of the forest. We still need them." My protest falls on three sets of deaf ears.

Cassius kneels to rummage through the saddlebag. He pulls out a waterskin and shakes it. Only a small amount of liquid sloshes around inside. When he stands and faces me, he says, "We need to feed."

"Are you sure it was necessary to release them so soon?" Lawrence grumbles.

So soon? Releasing them was the plan?

"What about the horses?" I ask dumbly. This was my journey, and yet I seem to be the only one unaware of the plan.

"They were never going to go into the forest with us."

I frown. "I don't understand."

Della steps up between us, hands on her hips. "You mean to say with all the talking you two have done, you never thought to explain?"

"Explain what?"

She turns a pitying glance on me. "The different witch covens put wards up around the forest. Horses tend to spook at mingling magics."

Lawrence stands several yards back with his arms crossed over his chest. His expression says what no one else speaks aloud. I was wholly unprepared when I decided to undertake this mission.

How could I have known where to begin? I blindly stumble through the world of vampires at Nightwich. My naivety has nearly killed me more than once because I know nothing of the world outside of Littlemire.

My companions were never meant to come along, though I am grateful they did. Della has her own agenda. Lawrence is Alaric's closest friend, and Cassius... to save me from Elizabeth's wrath.

After they finish feeding, emptying all but half of one waterskin, we walk the rest of the distance to the forest's edge.

Warm air breathes out of the forest before we set foot inside. Soon, sweat dampens the inner layer of my fur-lined clothes which are now too warm to be comfortable.

The men lead the way, but Della lags several paces behind, panting by the time we enter the shelter of trees. Cassius's shirt clings to his back, a dark line of sweat running down his spine.

"How is it this warm so far north in the middle of winter?" I ask.

"Magic. Obviously," Lawrence answers tersely. "The barrier dampens our connection to our demons making us weak."

I fall back to walk beside Della. She seems to be struggling the most.

"How are you holding up?" I ask.

"I'm not used to the lack of strength."

I take her pack and sling it over my shoulder. She looks as if she'll protest but changes her mind. It doesn't matter that she wouldn't do the same if our roles were reversed. I would rather she not slow us down.

"This place isn't so much of a forest as it is a bog," Lawrence complains.

The heavy humid air is filled with the lingering scent of rain mixed with wet wood and damp moss. Even if the loam is muddy from a recent rainfall, this forest is anything but a bog.

Della's dark eyes blaze with irritation. "You didn't need to come along at all."

I straighten my spine and tune them out, not wishing to get between them. They have barely left each other's side, and yet, she seems to resent his presence, and he remains cold toward her. As long as it doesn't slow us down or keep us from getting to the witch, I don't care.

The trees are thick and gnarled, growing unnaturally close together as if fighting to claim the same space. Anything faster than walking would be nearly impossible. Some only have the width of a man between them but bend and tangle together halfway up. We duck under branches and skirt around massive trunks, doing our best to stick to the thin strip of land that is the flattest and least tangled in vines.

After another hour into the trek, we are surrounded by swamps on both sides. Decaying vegetation and something rotten churns my stomach, and with every breath, I can taste it on my tongue.

Now, this is a bog.

The water and mire slosh over our path in wide patches, ankle-deep in some places and midcalf in others. It sucks at our feet as if trying to claim us.

I glance toward Cassius, but his gaze remains locked straight ahead. A muscle ticks in his jaw, betraying the otherwise cool exterior.

It's a relief when we leave the swamps behind for solid ground again. Dropping the two bags, I sag against a tree, using it to hold me up.

"Della, come with me," Cassius orders. She scrunches her nose but obeys without comment. "Lawrence, stay with Clara. I want to scout ahead."

I sit on a wide, protruding root, glad to be off my aching feet. Lawrence remains standing across from me, his spine as straight as a needle. He studies me with a hate-filled glance.

I pull out a wrapped piece of teek and break off a small portion, then place the rest back into the bag. Tying Della's bag to mine, I nibble on the flat, dense cake and do my best to ignore his stare.

"Don't get your hopes up," Lawrence says. "You have nothing to offer the oracle."

I snap my head up just as I bite through the chunk of bread. It crumbles, and half my meal drops to the ground. "Excuse me?"

"As much as I would like for your little plan, or—

non-plan as it were—to work, you do need to be realistic."

I take a swig from my waterskin, deciding not to respond to the bait. However, it seems he can't stop himself as he continues on, trying to wound me with his words like picking at a scab.

"I wonder… If I confessed my love for you too, would you drop this silly quest and return to Nightwich with me?"

My anger flares, and I'm on my feet in a flash, cutting the distance between us in three strides. I yank the dagger from the sheath and pin my forearm to his chest. The sharp point presses into his jaw without breaking the skin.

"I'm not here to prove myself to you, Mr. Harkstead," I say through gritted teeth. "But don't even think about sabotaging me."

"Or what, *slayer*? You'll kill me, too?" Lawrence says in a mocking tone loaded with meaning. "I will only be another notch on your belt."

His lip curls when my pressure on the dagger eases from the sharp accuracy of his words.

"Don't call me that," I hiss.

He arches a brow. "Call you what? A slayer? But you *are* a slayer, Clara. It is your title, and you've earned it."

"You can keep your titles." I clench my jaw. "Why did you come along?"

His green and gold hazel eyes glint with a mixture of mischief and malice as he debates his next words. "Alaric is my friend. You are not the only one who cares about him."

"Is that the only reason?"

"Partially," Lawrence says honestly. "I have my suspicions… I don't want to see him hurt, not by the likes of you."

Suspicions?

Taken aback, I release him and move away, putting distance between us. He rubs his neck where the dagger pricked him and scoffs when he doesn't find a single droplet of blood.

"You've taken it upon yourself to act as my chaperone because you think I will betray him." It isn't a question.

"Can you blame me, Clara?" Lawrence asks darkly.

"Why would I try to break the compulsion if I thought for a second that I could stand the idea of leaving him?" I ask, barely above a whisper.

"Guilt over what you took from him," he offers.

And me.

The unspoken words hang in the air between us.

Clearly, Lawrence has even more to say because he continues, "I see the way you are with Cassius. It wasn't that long ago when you acted nearly as affectionate with Alaric. Now Cassius has also declared his love for you."

So, he and Della did overhear our conversation.

"You talk as though you understand, but you don't. No matter what I say or do, you only see what you want."

There are times when Lawrence is more neutral toward me than others, but this is one of his harsher moments.

Ignoring me, Lawrence continues, "Alaric has been through enough... Does he need a broken heart on top of everything he's already endured?"

My face burns with embarrassment as I sheathe the dagger.

I want to tell him that he's wrong, that I'm doing this for Alaric. How can he not see that? I should point out that I had no say in Cassius becoming my new master.

But I don't. Words stick in my throat like cold honey.

"Tell me, Clara. How long before you forsake him in favor of another vampire who begs you for your affections? How much power must we have to catch your eye?"

I stumble back like he slapped me, mouth agape.

Regardless of how much of a demon's ass he can be, I trust him with my life. But there is still a limit to how much I can take.

The other two vampires round the bend, effectively ending our conversation.

"There's only one way through this forest," Cassius says. "We should keep going. We'll lose light even earlier in here. At the rate we're moving, I suspect we will reach the witch's ground in another day or—"

Spinning on my heel, I snatch up my pack and fling it over my shoulder, then stomp past Cassius and Della.

I haven't gone more than a few steps before a strange clicking sound stops me in my tracks. The small hairs on the back of my neck stand on end. Slowly, I turn to look back at the others, chatting quietly as they shoulder their bags.

My vampire companions all freeze. And despite the warmth of the forest, a chill races down my spine as the clicking directly above my head grows louder.

CHAPTER FIFTEEN

CLARA

I LIFT MY GAZE, BARELY TILTING MY HEAD TO LOOK AT the creature. From the corner of my eye, all I can see is a fiery orange face and long, razor sharp teeth, too close for comfort.

Unholy demon shit... what part of the Otherworld did this creature spring from?

Cassius extends his hand. "Clara," he says, calm and slow. "Walk toward me, and don't make any sudden movements."

I want to ask what the animal is, but the thin line of his lips and flaring nostrils tell me to keep quiet. He's not looking at me but beyond, at the space over my head.

Slowly, shifting my weight off my right foot, I inch it forward.

An itch starts at the back of my neck, prickling until I can't bear it. I shift, ready to turn.

"Don't," he warns. Then to the others, he orders, "The two of you stay back… no matter what happens."

I take a step, then another. With my heart pounding in my chest, I fight the instinct screaming for me to run—not that my shaking legs could carry me far.

The toe of my boot hits a small rock, sending it skidding across the path.

A heavy thud shakes the ground, knocking me off balance. Then a deep, rumbling snarl vibrates through my bones.

Cassius's eyes go wide just before the force of what feels like a large man rams into my back. I collide with Cassius as he rushes forward to catch me.

The creature shoves me again, and Cassius and I tumble to the ground. He twists, ending up on top. Then rolling to the side, he takes the creature with him.

Shimmying out of the straps, I turn toward him just in time to see a foxlike creature four times the size it should be pounce on him. Cassius raises the arm, and the beast clamps down. He grunts, using his other hand to push at its face. The creature is all muscle. Drool hangs from its snarling mouth.

Demons and saints... what is that?

It's large. Impossibly large, with the body of a fox. Many of its features have strange proportions. The ears are too tall and wide, and the eyes that take up half its face glow demon red. A black stripe runs down its back and over the tail. The massive paws are an uneven black up each leg. The animal is covered in what looks like dried, muddy swamp water. Unlike any woodland creature I've ever seen, two short horns produced from its head curl back like that of a goat.

Demons and saints. The stories about animals mixed with demons *are real?*

Rearing back its head, the swamp fox lunges at his face. Cassius barely manages to get out of the way before it strikes.

Terror closes in on my throat and seizes my muscles. I can hardly breathe as I watch the demon-sent beast attack. Pushing my fear down, I pull the dagger out.

With the different magics in the forest diminishing their powers, the vampires aren't used to being weak.

But I am. I can fight through the fatigue.

Cassius's gray eyes find me as I roll to my stomach and shift the dagger to my left hand as I rise into a low crouch.

I will only get one chance.

He nods. Taking hold of the beast's ear, he yanks hard and offers up his injured arm. It roars in his face, then clamps down. Blood soaks its muzzle and drips all over Cassius.

I leap for the creature's horn and hold tight as I crash into its muscle and rancid smelling fur. The swamp fox lifts its head, jerking Cassius with it as it tries to dislodge me.

I hook my legs around the neck for leverage and press against the side of its face.

When I see my reflection in the red orb, I aim and plunge the dagger into the massive eye, down to the hilt.

The swamp fox shrieks. The sound is earsplitting and so much worse than any noise I've ever heard from a demon. It bucks, and I loosen my legs, managing to dangle from the horn. I twist the blade, then rip it out.

Cassius kicks the swamp fox off as I let go, landing hard on the ground. The beast stumbles to the side, swaying. It collapses in a heap sending a shudder through the ground.

No one moves or utters a word for a long moment as we wait to see if it's truly dead. The belly rises and falls unevenly a few times, then doesn't move again.

Panting, I kneel before Cassius, my hands

hovering over the shredded muscle of his damaged arm. He's losing a lot of blood. My gaze flicks to his pale face, and he offers me a weak smile.

I use the dagger to cut his sleeve out of the way, then slice a strip of fabric from the edge of my blouse to bind his arm. His eyes are unfocused as I wrap the wounds. It isn't until I finish that he snaps out of his daze.

Shifting to sit, he winces when he jostles his arm. "It's been longer than I can remember since I've needed help for an injury."

"Does it hurt?"

"Not too much," he says. Cassius tries to push to his feet, stumbling slightly. I place his uninjured arm over my shoulder and help hoist him up. "Thank you, little bird. You really are turning out to be a remarkable slayer." He eyes the swamp fox. "Of both vampires and beasts."

"You are mistaken. I am no slayer. I am only a human," I say with a laugh. "With the strangest of allies."

He holds his arm, bearing the brunt of his injuries to his chest as we make our way to the slain creature, slowly converging on it.

Lawrence and Della join us wordlessly. Its muzzle is curled into a permanent snarl as if ready to attack, even in death. The fur is matted in several areas, and the ears are twice as big as they should be for a creature its size.

The ground trembles and cracks. Everyone jumps back as the animal sinks, the ground pulling it under like quicksand. The forest appears to be reclaiming... or consuming it. It's hard to say.

"Now why in the Otherworld is a human escorting and protecting three vampires in my forest?" a dry, frail voice asks from behind.

I spin and gape. Standing in the middle of the path is an old woman. She looks as though a strong wind would knock her over and break several bones. Her back is hunched, more so on one side than the other, and the skin of her face is lined with deep wrinkles. Covering most of her body is a heavy brown cloak, buttoned from hem to neck. The hood pulled over her head shades her eyes but not her sharp nose or thin lips, parted to reveal an amused smile.

Cassius steps forward.

The woman waves a hand and turns her back, dismissing him. "You may speak with me inside."

"There's no shelter anywhere near here," Della protests. "We scouted the area earlier."

The woman chuckles. "Isn't there?"

The four of us exchange glances, dumbstruck. Each step the woman takes looks almost painful. She couldn't possibly travel far in her condition, yet she wasn't in the area minutes ago.

My vampire companions don't seem inclined to indulge her. I find it too coincidental that a frail woman appeared out of nowhere and is under the impression that there's shelter nearby.

Sprinting, I scoop up my bag and hurry to follow a few steps behind her. Then after a moment, three sets of boots treading over the loam, trail at my back.

We travel down the singular path I was about to take before the demonic swamp fox attacked. But when we pass two large trees, I stop mid-stride, nearly stumbling.

What in the Otherworld?

A clearing opens before us that should have been visible from where we fought. The area is encircled by trees growing so close together it would be impossible to enter from anywhere else. A cozy cabin with lazy smoke curling from the chimney and candlelight flickering through the windows sits in the center. It smells like spring, with fresh grass and the warm perfume of flowers. This should be impossible.

The woman doesn't stop until she reaches the door. With a wave of her hand, it swings open. Climbing the two steps onto her rickety porch, I stop and face her.

She pushes her hood back, revealing grayish-blue

eyes so pale they almost look white. A long, black braid with silver strands woven through spills over her shoulder and hangs down nearly to the ground.

"You're the oracle witch."

She shrugs. "Come, child, let us sit by the fire. Standing in doorways is no place to speak of business."

I look over my shoulder and jerk my head for the others to follow.

Herbs and jars hang from the rafters so low I have to duck and weave to avoid getting them tangled in my hair. Inside, it smells of warm wood, herbs, spices, and fresh bread.

The cabin is small, a fireplace to the left as we enter, a small bed directly across from it, and a single table with two chairs near the back separating the central area from what looks to be the kitchen with a ratty curtain pinned to the side. A fire crackles in the hearth, warming the space.

There's a thin workbench along the wall with an open book, some equipment that looks too small to use for cooking, and several tiny jars. Above is a hanging shelf secured to the wall above the workbench with books at every angle and bobbles decorating the ends.

"Sit wherever you like," the oracle says.

I walk further into the room, too anxious to keep still. My companions remain close to the door.

"How is this possible, witch? We're nowhere near the heart of the forest," Cassius demands.

"My name is Ophelia, *vampire*," she says sharply. "And I did not live this long by staying in one place. Now, mind your tongue if you wish to stay. Your kind is not welcome here."

"Please," I say, moving to stand between them. A feud will not help me get what I've come for. "He didn't mean anything by it."

Ophelia raises a brow. "First, you save him and now, you defend him?"

I look back at the three vampires. "They're my friends. I couldn't have made it this far without them."

"Mmm," she hums to herself. "That does not speak highly of your abilities."

I wave a hand behind me and gesture for them to sit—or at least not cause trouble. Della takes a seat at the table with her back to the wall. The men sit on the floor, their backs against the wall near the bed.

"I need your help."

Ophelia regards me for a painfully long moment, then with a grunt, she says, "Wait here."

She turns and hobbles to the back room. I look at Cassius, wondering what he makes of all this, but his expression is carefully neutral. Clinking dishes come from the other room.

Moments later, she returns with a pot and several cups on a tray and sets it on the table. She seems sturdier in her home, her steps longer and stronger. The oracle pours tea into each cup. The vampires take theirs and sip obediently. I accept mine but hold it with both hands, eager to get down to business now that we've found the oracle witch.

"I was told—"

"There will be time enough for that later." Ophelia cuts me off as she takes a seat in the remaining chair.

My skin crawls, feeling each and every passing second. I want to get the spell and return to Alaric as soon as possible. To keep from shaking her until she hands over the spell, I brush my thumb back and forth over the coarse texture of the cup. Offending her will not help.

Ophelia sips her tea and motions for me to do the same. I throw it back in a single gulp and remain rooted in place and silent, waiting for permission to begin.

She finishes her drink, sets the empty cup on the table, then stands. "Come, child, we will speak without ears to listen."

I toss a furtive look back at the others before following her into the kitchen.

The ratty curtain slides over the doorway, blocking us from view as if it will somehow prevent their sensitive hearing from picking hearing every word.

With barely enough room for us to stand in the kitchen without embracing, my backside ends up pressed against a wood-burning stove—which is thankfully cold. The oracle stands with her back to a counter cover. Precarious stacks of dishes that look like they might topple over at any moment cover the surface.

Ophelia waves her arm, speaking words I don't know, but there is power in every syllable she utters.

Magic crackles all around us, electric, like the air a moment before lightning strikes. A nearly transparent shield forms over the doorway, glistening in the dim lantern light like a soap bubble.

CHAPTER SIXTEEN

CLARA

"I NEED YOUR HELP," I SAY AGAIN.

"Mmm," she hums, gaze narrowed. Her wrinkled skin nearly swallows up her eyes. "I can see that. No one seeks me out unless they are desperate with no other options."

"No one?" I ask.

Ophelia chuckles. "The price of magic is steep, far more than any ordinary mortal can afford, and higher still than most vampires are willing to pay." She scratches her dry cheek with cracked nails. "What could possibly be worth the payment for you?"

I swallow the lump of fear lodged in my throat. I still have nothing to offer. "I need to free someone from the queen's compulsion."

Her eyes glitter with curiosity. That has to be a good sign.

"Who exactly needs to be rescued from her clutches?"

Inhaling deeply, I say, "The crown prince."

The oracle throws her head back and laughs. "Why would a human try to save the prince of vampires from his fate?"

I fight back the surge of panic threatening to take over and lift my chin in determination. "No one deserves to be trapped that way. I—" I stop myself from saying too much. "I was told you could help."

Her lips press into a tight line. "Who would know to send you to me?"

"It isn't important," I say.

She knows what I want—that's all that matters. Would anyone willingly help someone sent to them by a demon?

A wrinkled hand shoots out and tangles in my hair, dragging my head down with a painful tug until the scent of mint leaves fills the space between us.

"Who sent you?" she half-growls, twisting harder until my neck is at a painful angle, and I think she might rip a fistful of strands out by the root.

"Varin… Varin sent me." The demon's name comes out breathy and strained.

Ophelia releases me. Her expression gives

nothing away. I stumble back, catching myself on the iron stove. My breath catches as I wait for her decision.

"A human traveling with vampires who would rescue their prince and consorts with powerful demons. That is an unlikely combination I did not see coming." She talks quietly, more to herself than to me. Her pale eyes dart back and forth as if calculating things I can't even begin to guess at. Finally, she heaves a sigh and says, "There is nothing I can do for you. You've wasted your time."

Ice fills my veins. Varin sent me to her... all for nothing. "Why?" I demand.

She scoffs. "You expect a lot, child. To act against the queen is no small thing—and you ask me to do so without payment."

"Anything," I say hastily. "Name your price, and I will gladly pay it."

White brows arch high on her forehead they almost touch her hairline. "*Anything?*"

Words stick in my dry throat, so I nod.

"That is a dangerous thing to offer," she warns.

Cassius said as much.

"I don't care."

"You may not like the price. I could ask for your sight, your mindless obedience, or the next fifty years of your life. Breaking a compulsion is a fairly simple spell but it takes a considerable amount of magic that is worth more than you can afford."

"Whatever you want, I will find a way to get it," I say bolder than I feel. "Alaric is worth it."

"Very well." Ophelia turns her back on me and searches through a cupboard. She grabs a small pouch and three jars of various sizes, dropping them inside with a clink. "You must gather four items. The bud of a night bloom. It's poisonous so take care not to touch it. One touch will paralyze you as its toxin enters your blood, liquefying you from inside. You will feel every agonizing second of it." Shoving the bag into my hands, she continues, "The tooth of a saaer."

"Saaer?" I frown. "You mean those swamp fox creatures?"

"They are called saaers." She looks unamused. "Now listen, the third is the eye of the redheaded seer witch."

I nearly choke in disgust. "You want me to take someone's eye? And wouldn't a seer know I'm coming for her?"

Ophelia grunts. "No. She can see the future of what might be for others but never herself. Be wary and do not harm any others, for she will see you then."

"You are more powerful than a greater witch. If these items can be gathered by someone like me, what is stopping you from collecting them yourself? Especially the eye."

"That may be, girl, but even I cannot win against them all. They would descend upon me like harpies sent from the Otherworld. That particular coven wiped mine out long ago, and now it's time for them to pay." Ophelia averts her gaze and quietly adds, "You have no idea what it is like to see another's fate and be helpless to change it."

Clutching the bag to my chest, I prompt, "And the final item?"

"That you will find when you are ready."

I want to throttle her and demand a straight answer. How can I bring back an item when it could literally be anything?

Something she said sparks my curiosity. "Have you seen Alaric's fate?" I ask.

She nods solemnly. "It is the sharpest I have ever seen. Your prince will be eternally at the vampire queen's side and loyal to none other. It is an inevitable conclusion, and nothing you do will alter the outcome. It would be best to go back home while you still have your life."

If that is true, then all of this is in vain, but quitting would shatter my heart. "Do you know my fate? Maybe—"

Maybe my fate is to change his.

"No. Some fates are not even mine to know." Ophelia pats my shoulder in a gesture of comfort.

Lowering my head, I squeeze my eyes shut. Even knowing his fate is set in stone, I can't sit back and watch him become Elizabeth's eternal prisoner. "I won't be able to live with myself if I don't do everything I can," I say.

The oracle nods as if she expected as much.

I repeat the list of items in my mind, planning the best way to gather them. The flower will be easiest, so I'll start there first, then the saaer. And somehow, I'll manage to find the witch and—I shudder—pluck her eye. My stomach churns, I don't want to think about those details until necessary.

"And these items are my payment?" I ask.

"These are but a small portion, but the final item will cover the remainder."

With all of the talk about the price of her magic, these items seem a paltry sum. My shoulders droop as something occurs to me. "Will I need to gather the ingredients for the spell as well?"

"Enough questions. Now go and hurry back."

"Thank you," I say, turning away.

Her frail hand grabs my wrist with surprising strength, stopping me. "Once you step into the forest, you will not be able to find your way back until you have collected everything or have failed."

I nod, and she waves her arm, filling the small space with her power until the barrier dissipates with an audible pop.

Della sits at the table, staring unseeing into the cup cradled in her palms and Lawrence stands behind her, hands clasped at his back as he watches the flames dance in the hearth.

Cassius cradles his arm to his chest. He lowers it and flinches when he moves too fast. Rising to his feet, he takes an uncertain step, green eyes questioning.

Turning to the oracle witch, I ask, "Can you help him?"

"Choose, girl," she says blandly. "You can help only one vampire with the aid of my magic, and you should be grateful I have allowed that much. There is not an endless supply at your disposal for frivolous things."

I glance at Cassius. His injury is hardly frivolous, and it will heal soon enough. However, Alaric will remain trapped without the oracle's spell.

His wounds have started to bleed through the makeshift wrap. A pang of guilt twists. I can't leave him like this when he was hurt protecting me.

"What would it cost for fresh bandages and a needle with thread?"

Her eyes glint with amusement. "That, my girl, you can have for free."

I cross the room to Cassius as the witch returns to the kitchen.

"Sit," I order, pointing to the floor.

He starts to protest but stops at the narrowing of my eyes—or perhaps because of the worry seeping in.

Cassius takes a seat, crossing his legs, and holds his arm out. I carefully unravel the scrap of my shirt. Della places a bowl of hot water with a sponge to my right. Then I set to work.

I can feel the weight of everyone in the room watching. My hands shake as I clean around the torn skin, squeezing water over the deep gashes to flush out bits and pieces of dirt.

Before I lose my nerve, I pick up the needle and thread placed atop a stack of fresh bandages. Tension works its way up the muscles in my back.

After several attempts, the thread finally slides through the eye of the needle. Hovering over the first slice, my forehead prickles with sweat. I glance up at Cassius. His face is void of emotion as he continues to hold his arm out for me.

I grimace as the needle pierces his flesh, then sew the first loop, tugging lightly to pull the skin together. He hisses and bares his fangs but falls back into his blank expression almost as quickly.

Cassius doesn't move or speak again as I continue to stitch each wound. He might as well be made of stone.

Sitting back on my heels when I finish, I examine my work. It isn't as nice as I would like, but it will do until we are out of the forest and he can heal quickly. At least the bleeding has stopped.

I look to him for approval. Cassius rotates his arm with a lift of his brows.

"I'm willing to bet that your sister was the seamstress in your family," he says dryly.

My mouth falls open.

Lawrence snorts with laughter from behind. "You can all let me die if that's the quality of treatment I'll be receiving. What a shame, Cassius, to have such crooked scars on your flawless skin."

Della covers her mouth doing a poor job stifling her amusement.

Heat floods my cheeks. I fling the sponge into the bowl, sloshing water over the rim, and move to stand. Cassius reaches out to stop me. His fingers slide up the back of my hand and curl lightly around my wrist.

I force myself to meet his eyes, humiliated by my lack of skill.

"Thank you, little bird," Cassius says quietly. He

lets his hand fall away and I straighten, taking everything into the back room.

CHAPTER SEVENTEEN

CLARA

Warm, golden light filters through the tops of the trees as I step out onto the porch. There are still a handful of hours before dark, even this close to the mountains.

"Remember, once you leave, you cannot return until you have the items or have failed," the oracle witch reminds me.

I nod. Armed only with my dagger and a satchel with three glass bottles, I step onto the stone path leading into the forest.

Cassius tries to follow, but before I can tell him to stay, he bounces off an invisible wall. He presses both palms against the barrier, and his eyes grow large.

"What is this?" he demands, turning on Ophelia with a snarl.

"This is a quest she must fulfill alone."

"She could die out there—"

"Then she dies," Ophelia cuts him off. "If she wants to save her vampire, she must do this without your help."

The space between my shoulders grows tight with tension. Della clasps a hand over her mouth, and even Lawrence looks mildly concerned. Their worry is wasted because I will not die.

I can't.

It is the sharpest I have ever seen. Your prince will be eternally at the vampire queen's side and loyal to none other. It is an inevitable conclusion, and nothing you do will alter the outcome. It would be best to go back home while you still have your life.

Even if the prophecy says I will fail, I refuse to give up.

I smile and wave, feigning confidence in my ability to complete this task. Then I step over the line from the stone path at the edge of the clearing and onto the soft loam of the forest.

Pausing, I look over my shoulder one more time. The clearing is gone and a tall tree now stands where I stepped off the path seconds ago. Beyond that, more forest stretches out, leaving no trace of the oracle witch's home. Thick fog billows up from nowhere, darkening the space between the trees at my back.

Adjusting the satchel over my shoulder, I make my way deeper into the forest, following the sound of a stream. The trees are farther apart now, more natural. It seems that Ophelia was guiding us to her from the moment we entered her domain.

If I hurry, we might be able to leave by morning. Even though it took two extra days to get here, there's a chance we can still return to Nightwich within the week.

I pick up my pace, weaving between trees and leaping over roots jutting out of the ground. By the time I reach the small stream feeding into the swamp, I have to stop and lean against a tree to catch my breath.

Flowers with three dark purple virulent petals and bright centers of cyan grow between tall grasses. The rich colors make everything else in this forest appear dull in comparison.

Squatting before a large bloom, I reach into the bag for the first vial and pop the cork with my teeth. A mouse-like creature with a tufted tail scampers by. When it sees me, it squeaks and bumps into one of the flower stocks in its attempt to get away. A single purple petal brushes its dark brown head. The mouse freezes between steps and then collapses onto its side.

Demons and saints...

My eyes widen in horror at the flower whose

poison worked too fast for my liking. In seconds, the rodent's fur and skin dissolve before my eyes, then the muscles and organs, until there's nothing left but bones—blackened as if scorched atop the layer of skin that rests against the forest floor.

Interesting.

I search the immediate area for something that will allow me to harvest the flower without touching it. My options are limited, but I eventually settle for testing a leaf.

I drop it right over the flower. It brushes against a petal as it falls, turning to ash before it even reaches the ground.

With my dagger, I prod at the flower. A light dusting of purple coats one side of the blade, but nothing happens. I bite the inside of my cheek and grin. The poison must only affect certain organic things, so the glass bottle should be impervious.

I lower the bottle opening over the bloom, leaving a small gap between the glass and dirt, and slice through the woody stem. Carefully tipping it right side up, I jam the cork into place, then wrap it in a leftover cloth strip before tucking it in alongside the other vials. I give the bag a good shake to make sure the glass won't clink when I move.

That wasn't so bad.

One item down, two—or I suppose—three to go.

I'm not sure how she expects me to collect the final item without a bottle, let alone know *what* it is.

But the mouse has given me an idea. I go in search of yet another flower and find one on a slightly raised patch of earth near the middle of the stream. After wading into the water, I carefully drag the tip of the blade over the petals until the fine purple dust coats both edges of the blade.

Now, for the second item on my list—the saaer.

Though, how common they are and how I will track one down, remains to be seen. It was pure chance we crossed paths with the last one. I suppose I could always wander around the forest until I find one, but that would waste time I don't have.

Striding back to the path, I decide that starting where I saw the last one is as good a place as any. Maybe there will be some trace that will help me find another. Boosted by how quickly I gathered the first item, I'm not bothered by the water that soaks the insides of my boots.

With dagger in hand, I run. My feet nearly fly over the ground. But like much of the way through the forest, the trees grow thick and dense again until there is only a single meandering path to follow.

After twenty minutes, I stop and look around. I don't know where I am, but straight ahead, deep claw marks have been gouged into a tree, shredding the bark off.

My breathing quickens. The claws that made those are easily twice the size of the saaer that attacked us.

"Hello?" I call out.

Familiar clicking sounds above in answer, followed by a heavy thud that shakes the ground behind me. I spin and lock eyes with a saaer so close I could almost reach out and touch its face.

This saaer is massive, with a back that must be over eight feet high. The one Cassius and I fought must have been young. Even then, we barely made it.

Unholy demon shit... I am going to die.

Curled black horns glint in the slowly dimming light. The saaer's nostrils flare sending hot, rancid breath washing over me in a nauseating wave that churns my stomach. Every instinct and nerve in my body tells me to run. But that would mean turning my back on this creature which would guarantee a swift and painful death.

I slide one foot back along the ground, slowly shifting my weight, then repeat, creating distance between us. A low, clicking noise emanates from its large throat.

My heel comes down on a small twig and the snap seems to ring out through the forest. The saaer lets out a ferocious growl and swings a meaty paw. I throw myself back and land hard, barely managing to avoid the razor-sharp claws.

Before I have a chance to roll away, it pounces and lands, caging me in with its legs. A thick string of drool hangs down from the creature's jowls, sliding closer to me.

I will my pulse to slow from the frantic roar in my ears.

Steady, Clara... I only have one chance.

The saaer screeches as the massive head rushes toward my throat. I roll to the side, bumping into the powerful limb just as the muzzle strikes the dirt, teeth scoring the earth. I lift the dagger and plunge it into the creature's neck with a twist.

The beast lifts a paw, long claws extended, and I lose my grip on the hilt. Blood, thick and dark, spills from the wound onto the ground beside me. I cover my face with my arms and wait for the saaer to rip me open.

When the forest falls silent, I chance a look. The saaer is frozen over me. The poison from the night bloom coated on the dagger has done its job.

The puddle of blood continues to grow, oozing closer. I scramble to get away, but the saaer's legs give out before I can make it far, and it collapses on top of me. The impact forces all the air from my lungs as it pins me from the chest down.

Wriggling and shoving to free myself does no good. It's far too heavy to move it on my own. I am well and truly trapped. I stop struggling so I can catch my breath while I figure a way out.

Think, Clara, think!

If I can't find a way out of this situation, the weight of the saaer will eventually crush me if some other creature looking for easy prey doesn't stumble across my path first.

Every breath is a struggle. I try sliding out sideways, which proves futile and a waste of energy. The dagger is still lodged in the beast's neck, out of reach, so that eliminates cutting my way free as an option.

After a while, I grow used to the weight on top of me and I can almost take a full breath again. I shift my leg, and… the saaer's body gives slightly under the pressure of my knee.

My heart hammers wildly.

What in the Otherworld?

Leveraging my arms between the ground and beast, I push and shove. I free myself inch by inch, until I am able to crawl out from under the saaer.

Pushing to my feet, I turn and gape. I can't tear my eyes away. The top half of the animal is nothing more than ash and blackened bones. The blight continues to spread, slowly disintegrating.

A back leg collapses, sending a chain reaction up the body of bones cracking and crumbling into dust.

The tooth.

Kneeling before the head, I pull the dagger free, ready to carve out the second item. Without hesitating, I bring the point down, slicing into the gums… and the skin turns to ash.

Shit, shit, shit!

There's still poison on the blade.

I stab the dagger into the earth and twist. The parts of the mouse that were touching the earth were untouched, so I hope my theory that it will clean my dagger is correct. *There's only one way to find out...*

I position the blade against a canine on the lower jaw. I carve against the muscle and bone.

Progress is far too slow for comfort. The poison-crumbling flesh inches closer. I plant a foot on the muzzle and grip the tooth with both hands, pulling with every ounce of strength I possess.

There's a cracking, then a snap as it gives way, sending me tumbling back. I roll to my stomach, clawing at the earth with my fingers, and bury the tooth in the dirt, packing as much as I can over it.

I pray to the demons and saints of the Otherworld that the poison didn't reach the root of the tooth.

I can't tear my eyes from the saaer until only ash and a partial pelt stretching out over the ground remain. Just a touch of the flower's poison on the dagger was enough to take down this large beast, barely leaving a trace that it ever existed.

After several minutes, I unearth the tooth and clean the moist dirt off with my sleeve. I take a moment to examine it, relieved to find the fang intact. It's large—three times as thick as my thumb and almost as long as my palm.

That was close. But with half the items already gathered, I'm hopeful I can return soon. A few hours of daylight remain before it will be too dark to continue.

Reaching for the satchel, I pull out an empty vial bottle and drop the tooth in with a clink. It rattles slightly as I twist a strip of cloth around it. Once I'm back on my feet, I sheathe the dagger and half-heartedly brush the loose dirt from my clothes.

I pace to help myself work through the next problem. The flower was easy, the saaer… less deadly than expected thanks to the night bloom's poison. All that is left is figuring out how to take the eye of a witch. Just the thought of it makes my stomach roil.

Closing my eyes, I focus on the soft sounds of the forest—trickling water, insects… and in the far distance, a song drifts through the strange warm air. The beautiful voice lulls me, urging me to rest for a bit.

Voice.

The word repeats loudly inside my mind, and my eyes snap open. The song is still there, but the light hold of the spell is broken. Thoughts race through my mind. Ophelia said the witch will see me if I harm others to get to her. Which means that if I want to get through this alive, I need a plan before I attempt anything.

Hiding will allow me to observe the seer witch long enough to make sure she's alone. If not, then I will wait until she is. That will also give me a chance to learn if she possesses other abilities on top of her sight.

The song gradually grows louder as the witch approaches.

I sprint away from the voice to the edge of the murky swamp. Smearing some of the mud on my exposed skin, I nearly gag. It smells of rotting flesh and stagnant water. The sound of singing continues to close in.

Quickly climbing the nearest tree, I crouch on a sturdy branch with enough leaves to hide me and clap a hand over my mouth.

Slow breath in. Slow breath out.

Forcing my aching lungs to relax, I keep the sounds of my breath near silent, gradually slowing my thundering heartbeat.

There is something peculiar about this quest. The saaer appeared almost immediately after the flower was packed in my bag. And now, just minutes after securing the tooth, the woman I can only assume is the witch I seek draws close.

It's too much to be a coincidence.

I don't have to wait long before she steps out from between trees. She wears a long white gown that flows around her in an ethereal wind, and her long, red hair hangs loosely down her back in wild curls.

She stops at the water's edge, her song breaking off. The silence that surrounds us is harsh and cutting. It feels cold.

Kneeling beside the stream, she dips a finger into the water and then traces lines across the surface as if writing or drawing—it's impossible to tell from my vantage point. I should have thought to gather another night bloom. Then again, if she is a skilled fighter, she could take the dagger and use it against me.

The witch's hand freezes in mid-motion. Her head snaps up, and she slowly scans the area. Then she's on her feet, and a single note reverberates through the forest.

I no longer have the element of surprise because along the water's edge is a partial footprint from my boot.

CHAPTER EIGHTEEN

CLARA

As the witch's hum increases, the dagger warms uncomfortably along my forearm through the sheath. Searing heat lances across my skin. I want to rip it off and fling it as far away as possible, but that would give away my position—and leave me without a weapon. Even if she doesn't know my exact location, there's no doubt in my mind that the witch knows I'm here.

The heat continues to intensify. I clutch my wrist, digging my fingers into the straps around my forearm as I grit my teeth against the blinding pain. Tears spill down my cheeks.

I draw the dagger and grip the hilt so tight my knuckles turn white. My palm feels as though my hand is too close to an open flame.

It's too much.

I leap down, landing in a crouch in front of her, and straighten. Only a few yards separate us. The burning spell dissipates as her bright, orange eyes land on me.

She grins wickedly. "It's about time you've come out of hiding, filthy human."

The bag slides from my hand as I pull my other arm back and bring the dagger forward. She lifts her hand, fingers splayed. An orb of power gathers in her palm—the same bright orange as her eyes. It grows to the size of an apple in a blink. It shoots out, hitting me in the chest before I can react.

The force sends me flying back. I land in the shallow edge of the swamp. Murky water splashes in every direction, then swallows me up as it settles again. I sit up, gasping for air.

"Who sent you?" the seer hisses. She reaches out and tangles her long fingers into the front of my shirt, dragging me toward her. She is nearly as strong as a vampire.

Pushing at her hand with little effect, I bite out, "No one sent me. I'm here on my own."

Slowly, I bring my other hand forward while I continue to struggle against her grip.

Divert her attention. I can almost hear Cassius's voice from our lessons.

I lift my arm up, but she lets go, dropping me back into the swamp. Her foot comes down hard on my chest again and again. Each kick sends my head underwater and the air from my lungs.

Then witch stomps into the water and squats over me. I sputter and look up into a youthful face. She leans in, giving me the perfect opportunity to strike. There's a pale scar over the bridge of her nose. She looks too human.

Our gazes remain locked. The hand clutching the dagger remains where it is underwater.

I saw her wield power—I know she is not human…. So why am I hesitating? I have killed vampires before, and they can look just as human.

Her eyes narrow. "You're nothing more than a weak, pathetic human." She tsks and shifts her weight as if to leave me in the mire to wallow in my failure.

If I don't make my chance now, everything I've gone through so far will be pointless, and Alaric will remain under Elizabeth's compulsion indefinitely.

I blow out a breath, and then her hands are around my throat.

The witch kneels, pinning my arm down with her foot. She pushes my head underwater. Her thin limbs are deceptively strong. Bone-like fingers tighten with bruising force.

I flail, desperately searching for a way to break her

hold. My lungs burn from lack of air. I dig my nails into her hand, but the witch's skin is hard as iron. The water is only knee-deep, but that's enough to drown as she holds me under.

The last of my strength leaches away as I cling to consciousness. I stop struggling. The seer witch's face becomes crystal clear through the unnaturally glassy surface as the water ceases to froth. Darkness bleeds in around the edges of my vision, but not enough to hide her true form.

Her skin is sallow. Scraps of flesh hang from her face, exposing bone and teeth within. Fangs jut up from her lower jaw, pressing into the skin of her cheeks. Her neck is exposed spine with strips of peeling muscle.

What skin she does have crawls and moves as if beetles skitter underneath. She is a corpse using a glamor to hide the horror of her nature.

I let my eyes close and let my body go completely limp. Her fingers tighten. I am moments away from passing out. Instinct urges me to fight her, screaming that I will die. It takes everything to resist, because if I don't, then she really will kill me.

Gradually, the witch's grip slackens. I let a few air bubbles escape my lips. Then finally, the long, skeletal fingers release my throat. Her weight lifts and her foot off my arm.

My eyes snap open. She kneels over me, gazing into the distance.

This time, I don't hesitate.

This time, I remember my mission.

I tighten my grip around the hilt and rise, knocking her off balance. The witch screeches, falling onto the muddy slash of land. Coughing up the dregs of water, I fling myself on top of her and bring my arm down hard.

The blade pierces her neck, sinking without resistance. Her cry cuts off with a thick gurgle, and then she goes still.

I gasp, sucking in deep lungfuls of warm, humid air against my scratchy throat. Shaking, I remove the dagger, grimacing at what's to come.

The mud inches up around the witch's body, pulling her into the earth.

Demon shit. The forest is reclaiming her.

Pressing the weapon's point to the corner of her eye, I work quickly. The moment I have what I need in hand, I scramble to dry land just as I begin heaving uncontrollably, losing what little there is in my stomach, still clutching both weapon and eye.

When there's nothing left, I sit back on my heels and sheath the dagger. I push to my feet and hurriedly fetch the last vial from the satchel. The eye is wet and the texture is unsettling in my hand. I try not to think or look as I secure it, then wrap it as I had the first two items.

Three small jars—each holding their intended item.

Tremors rack every muscle. I lean back against the tree and slide down to the ground, rubbing my bruised throat.

Even with the majority of what I need already gathered, success seems almost impossible. I don't know how I can possibly get the final item when I don't have a vial for it, let alone know *what* it is.

Ophelia said I'd find it when I was ready, but nothing stands out, nothing that there aren't a hundred others of—a hundred trees just like the hundreds of others I've passed. I'm ready. What could be worse than the saaer or witch that it wouldn't present itself just as quickly?

I rest and wait for the next thing to reveal itself as the others did. Time slips by, minute by minute. The forest remains quiet and still, as the daylight wanes.

No birds sing. No insects buzz. I am losing the last bits of light, and still, nothing presents itself. My heart sinks. I can't remain out here any longer.

Not knowing what else to do, I get up and jog back toward the clearing, desperately hoping to find what I need. No creatures or witches make themselves known. Nothing at all that could hold a clue.

With each step, I trip over roots, hiding in the shadows between trees. I scan every inch of the forest, looking for a clue… something—*anything*—that might lead me to the final item. As the three times before, the forest tightens around me until there is only one possible path.

Swallowing down a sob when I step onto the stone path, I race toward the cottage. My insides twist into knots, knowing what this means—I have failed.…

My only hope is that I misunderstood her, and she wants the first three things in hand before she reveals the final item.

I take the last steps from the path to the porch and bite down on my bottom lip. Then, with a steadying breath, I open the door and step through.

All three vampires stand and face me—eyes questioning, studying, and curious as to why I look like a drowned rat. But past them, Ophelia's smile slips from her face.

And it's that small detail that confirms my failure.

CHAPTER NINETEEN

CLARA

"There was nothing," I say.

Cassius speeds across the room and lifts my chin with a knuckle. I look up into his worried face. "You've been gone for two days, and didn't find anything?"

"Two days?" My brows crash together in confusion. "It was only a few hours."

He rubs his hands up over my arms. A crease forms across his forehead. "No, little bird," he whispers.

"Time is not always linear in the forest," the oracle says by way of partial explanation.

I can't focus on the magic of the forest or how it works. It doesn't matter, because I've lost more time than I can spare.

Three words reverberate in my mind with a dull pain: *I have failed.*

"It doesn't matter..." I murmur. "I—"

Ophelia cuts me off with a cough. When I turn my gaze on her, she motions me over. I shake off Cassius's hands, and walk around him.

"You have not failed yet, child," she says.

Yet? That one word revives my hope.

The oracle mutters strange words under her breath. Magic crackle on the air, making the hairs on my arms stand on end as it builds. My ears pop. The sound is punctuated by three heavy thuds from behind. I spin to find the vampires crumpled on the floor.

"What did you do?" I whisper.

Ophelia ignores my question. "The final item," she says, reaching into her wide sleeves, pulling a vial from one and a long blade, needle thin from point to hilt from the other, "is blood from the heart of a lover."

My pulse roars in my ears. "How can I offer you Alaric's heart when I am trying to save him?" I ask, fighting back the tears prickling behind my eyes. "If I knew he had to die, I would have ended him at Nightwich."

Otherworld damn Varin and this doomed quest.

My blood chills, turning my veins into icy rivers. The demon betrayed me.

The oracle says nothing, but her gaze slides toward Cassius's unconscious form.

"I don't understand," I say. My tongue feels thick and awkward in my mouth.

"He loves you even if he has forgotten what that means exactly." She stretches out her hand, offering the blade. When I don't take it, she shoves it into my palm and squeezes my fingers around it painfully. "His heart will do."

I take a step back in horror as the meaning of what she intends for me to do becomes clear. "He has nothing to do with this… we're not lovers."

Ophelia looks at me pityingly. "A lover does not need to have their feelings returned. I warned you before that the spell you seek comes with a heavy price. Now, finish what you came to do." She gestures to each unconscious vampire. "Any lover will do. It matters not whom they love, just that they love."

The three of them came with me this far to save Alaric, risking Elizabeth's wrath. And in return, I must kill one of them. This would be worse than the witch or the vampires who attacked me—worse than killing Rosalie—because I wouldn't just betray the one I murdered, I'd be betraying them all.

It wouldn't be self-preservation or even fear.

"They are not mine to give." I loosen my fingers. The dagger slips from my hand and clangs against the floor.

Ophelia scoffs. "The flower was not yours to harvest. The saaer was not yours to kill for its tooth. The witch was not yours to kill for her eye, and yet you did all those things." The witch throws her hands up. "You agreed to whatever price I asked—but I cannot help you if you are unwilling to pay. Magic demands sacrifice. To obtain anything worthwhile, you must give something of equal value in return."

I clutch the glass vial to my chest and stare horrified at Cassius. After everything he has done for me, how can I kill him while he lays unconscious on the floor?

"If you wish to save the man you love, you must pay what the magic demands." Ophelia picks up the thin blade and wraps my hand around the hilt.

No, it's my price to pay, not his. I can't take his life.

My heart plummets because if I don't, Alaric will remain under Elizabeth's power.

But he would rather die than be trapped.

My feet move of their own accord toward Cassius. I kneel at his side and roll him onto his back. Brushing my fingers over his forehead, I push loose strains of pale hair away from his face. He looks peaceful in this spelled sleep.

I squeeze my eyes shut. *Cassius... Alaric... can I bear to take either of their lives—to betray one of them?*

Slowly, I raise my shaking hand. The hilt feels cold and coarse against my palm.

There is no other choice.

"You are running out of time—you must make your decision now. Even I cannot keep three powerful vampires sedated for long."

A dark gleam shines in the oracle's eyes. Della stirs first. Then a soft groan comes from Lawrence. A finger on Cassius's hand twitches then another, stretching out.

"Can you guarantee that Alaric will be free of the compulsion if I give you what you want?" I ask, barely above a whisper. My stomach roils.

"Yes."

Cassius's eyes flutter open. His gaze cuts to the dagger raised above his chest, lips parting in shock. Before he can utter a word or move to stop me, I drive the blade down.

The breath leaves my lungs as I stare at the blade protruding halfway out of my chest. It doesn't hurt as much as I expected. It's more like being poked with a sewing needle.

I press harder. The agony finally rears up as the blade slides closer to its target. Tears spring up, sliding down my cheeks. I try to scream but can only manage a strangled and broken cry.

The second the sharp point, pierces my heart, ice and fire explode in my chest. I gasp—or, rather, I try to—my lungs no longer work.

I rip the dagger out, letting it slip from fingers that refuse to work a second longer. Ophelia catches it in a smooth, swift motion. Cassius reaches for me as my legs give way, and we fall together in a tangled heap.

His palm is warm on my face, nearly scorching as he presses his hand to my chest, trying to stanch the bleeding. Mouth moving with the shape of my name, Cassius scowls, somehow managing to look both worried and furious.

His features shift in and out of focus, and then everything turns black.

Something is wrong. It hurts to breathe. My body is too heavy, and my heart aches. I blink my eyes open. Fire crackles in the hearth on the other side of the room. A blanket is tucked up to my chin, pinning my arms to my sides.

"Alaric," I say his name, and it's barely more than a rasp of air.

I close my eyes again, squeezing them tight. A tear finds its way out. It sears a trail down the side of my face. *He is lost to me.*

There's a shuffling sound and a clatter of cups, followed by soft murmurs.

My memory is hazy. I look around at the unfamiliar cabin, unable to remember where I am or how I got here. I shift, working to free my arms from the restraining covers.

Della is at my side in an instant, sliding an arm under my shoulders to help me sit. She repositions the pillow behind me.

"Move slowly," she says.

I wince at the sharp pain in my chest. It burns, and the skin pulls taut and uncomfortable.

"What happened?" My voice is raspy and painful.

I look around at the small living area. Lawrence sits at a small table, drumming his fingers over the surface.

Della presses her lips into a thin line, looking to Cassius for an answer as he exits the kitchen with the oracle on his heels. His face darkens then he rushes over, guiding Della out of the way to take her place. His hands are all over my face and neck, feeling for what I assume is a fever. I'm too tired to put up a fight.

"You were injured, little bird," he says softly as his hand hovers over my chest. "Rest more."

Cassius reaches down and picks up a cup, bringing it to my lips. Delicate floral notes waft up from wisps of steam.

"Drink," he commands.

I have no choice but to drink as he tilts the cup, or it will end up down my front. The taste is familiar, reminding me of the sleeping draughts mother made for Kitty and me when we were sick. In moments, my muscles are heavy with exhaustion, and I give into it.

Cassius adjusts me to lay back. Della appears over his shoulder, glowering before I can thank him. She grabs his arms and jerks him away just as my eyes slide closed.

"You are a bastard, Cassius," Della scolds in a harsh whisper I don't think she intends for me to hear. "You should have told her."

"She will find out later, after she heals."

Find out what? I want to ask, but I'm swallowed up by unconsciousness once more.

CHAPTER TWENTY

CLARA

Alaric stands across from me in the dark void. He lifts his head, bright sapphire eyes glittering. Then, rushing over, he wraps me up in his arms, placing kisses on my forehead, eyes, and lips. Pulling back just enough to look at me, he says, "I fear I have not given you enough credit, my dear Clara."

"Is this real?" I ask. Reaching up, I skim my fingers across his brow and over the familiar planes of his face.

He looks at his hand and flexes it then moves his arm.

"It feels good to be in control of my body again." His voice is full of wonder, but it breaks my heart to know how trapped he has been.

Then his mouth crashes back down on mine,

kissing me desperately. It holds all the anger and crushing passion we shared every time I tried to cut him. I gasp as his breath steals mine. His fangs scrape the delicate flesh of my lip, and I taste the sharp tang of blood.

It is the kiss that stole my heart.

He pulls back, eyes bright in the dark. A thin line of red rings his irises. "You were gone for so long from my dreams, I couldn't summon you. I thought you had forsaken me, given up your impossible quest... or that you died," he admits, voice cracking at the end.

I cling to him, wrapping my arms around his neck and pressing myself against him as tightly as possible, wanting nothing more than to be part of him. "You are a fool, Alaric," I whisper against his chest. "I will never give up on you. Never."

"You've been gone a long time." He lifts his head and looks off to the side as if he can hear or see something that I can't.

"It feels like forever," I agree. "I've been gone a few days more than expected, but we will still have a month and a half."

His head snaps in my direction, brows furrowed. "Clara, it's been longer than that. The coronation is just over five weeks away. Otherworld take me, I wish you could... but you cannot save me."

"I refuse to stop trying. What would you do if I was in your place?"

"I would tear the world apart," he says honestly. One corner of his mouth ticks up in a rueful smile.

"Exactly."

"It is in the nature of vampires to be selfish. I would see others destroyed to have you by my side." Alaric laughs softly. "I have held onto my humanity for nearly two hundred years, and within months you have inspired me to embrace what I am. You are the air my lungs demand. And there is no freedom without you."

Heat races up my neck to burn my cheeks at his proclamation, and yet my heart thunders, reveling in his sweet words.

Gathering me up in his arms, he kisses me. I melt into him, missing his touch, his voice, his presence. It's a kiss I want to get lost in… a kiss I would die for.

White hot pain pierces flares through my chest. I pull back and press a hand over my heart, then in the next instant, it's gone.

Everything comes flooding back. The excruciating pain, the items the oracle sent me after, the final one being the heart of a lover… And I had chosen my own.

How am I alive?

You don't nearly die for someone you don't love

with every fiber of your being. This is real… it was always real. And I should have told Alaric the last time we were together.

But the past is written and cannot be undone.

"You truly are a slayer, my dear Clara, a slayer of vampires, a conqueror of hearts. You have slain me long before I realized."

"I hate that title," I say, frowning. I'm not sure what he means by that, but it doesn't matter. There have been so many lost chances, and I refuse to lose another. Setting my jaw, I say, "I have to tell you something."

His mouth crashes down on mine again, silencing me, but I break away.

"Alaric, I—"

He presses the tip of his finger to my lips. "Not here," he says. "I want you to keep your promise first, and then you can say everything."

I bite down a growl of frustration as the need to tell him how I feel rises to my lips, demanding to be released.

"I still don't know if this is real," he admits. "I would hate to hear the words I long for only to be shattered when they never come once you wake me from this spell."

I sit up with a gasp. My heart cracks because Alaric has slipped through my fingers again. I'm back in the oracle's tiny cabin.

Della shifts on the foot of the bed. As she watches me, head canted to the side, the corners of her lips tug into a frown.

My brows crash together, not understanding her expression. "What's wrong?"

At my words, she moves, standing and adjusting the pillow so I can sit up. She pulls back the collar of my shirt, exposing a thick cloth over my chest.

"You've woken up so many times after the initial…" She trails off, clearing her throat. "But you always immediately fell back to sleep," she explains while her fingers set to work, removing the cloth and wiping off the dried poultice underneath, revealing a bright pink scar. The skin is puckered and raw.

I open my mouth to speak, but flounder, unable to find the right words.

"Lie back down," Della says as she smears a fresh poultice layer and places a clean cloth over it.

I push her hands away and sit up, much to her annoyance.

Cassius barges through the front door, eyes wild and bringing cool air with him. He kicks the door shut, and as soon as his eyes land on my face, he rushes over, towering above me.

"How am I still alive?" I ask them.

Cassius crosses his arms over his chest. "That is a good question." He bares his teeth. "You are a demon's damned idiot for trying to kill yourself. I would shake some sense into you if you weren't already so close to the Otherworld's door."

His anger feeds my own, and I'm on my feet in an instant. Cassius reaches out to push me back down to the bed, but I sidestep.

"Should I have chosen you then—thanked you for your troubles with a blade through your heart?"

Spinning on my heel, I march over to where the oracle stands before the messy bench stacked with books and bobbles. She works with wax and herbs and symbols, her fingers moving deftly as she speaks words I don't know in a low tone.

"The closer the heart to you, the more powerful the magic," she mutters under her breath.

"How am I alive?"

Her movements still, and though she says nothing, Ophelia looks sidelong at Cassius. My gaze follows her. He hasn't moved other than to face me, with arms still crossed over his chest and lip curled up in a vicious scowl.

"That should have killed me," I say when no one answers.

Ophelia squints, scrunching up her wrinkled face. "Do you long to die so badly?"

I take a step back. "Of course not."

"Then why are you so insistent?"

"I want to understand what happened," I say quietly.

The oracle plucks an empty vial and pours a deep blue liquid into it then speaks more words. She wraps it in a cloth and holds it out to me. I reach for the vial, but she snatches her hand away.

"This will not solve your problem."

I swallow. "Once he's no longer compelled, I can figure out how to fix everything else."

Ophelia nods. "Your lives are now tied together," she says. My mind goes instantly to Alaric, but she continues, "Magic demands a price, and that was the price offered to save your life."

Not Alaric then.

My pulse drums in my head as I turn toward Cassius. He looks struck, pain etched into his expression.

Tied? We're tied? I don't understand.

"What have you *done*?"

Cassius is across the room in less than a heartbeat, sneering. "No, little bird, what have *you* done? What choice did you give me? You would be dead otherwise, and then your precious Alaric would have killed me for allowing it to happen." His face softens. "You cannot save him if you are in the Otherworld."

I snap my mouth shut. Any retort I might have had dies on my tongue.

He's right, of course.

But *tied*… to *him*?

The thought fills me with unease. I've only recently started thinking of him as my friend and true ally, and now we are tied to each other in a way I don't understand.

I have no idea what this will mean for Alaric and me, but first things first, I must break Elizabeth's compulsion. Then we can figure everything else out together.

Ophelia clasps my hands in hers, pressing the vial into my palm. It seems to pulse with the heartbeat of magic.

"You are young still, new to the ways of the world around you. You do not grasp the depth and power of magic just yet." She pats my hands. "Have your vampire drink this, and the compulsion will be broken. He will never again be compelled by anyone."

"Thank you," I whisper.

"Be warned—this will not protect him from other magics."

I nod. The warning falls away as I stare down at the dark vial in my hand that will save Alaric. "What do I owe you?"

"You wish to pay more than you already have?" Her bushy brows shoot up her forehead nearly to her hairline.

"No… I mean, I want to pay what I owe for this."

Ophelia smiles and pats my cheek with her dry, leathery hand. "You have paid your price. Now go, save your prince."

Hurrying to my bag sitting against the bed, I kneel down and rummage through it.

"What are you doing?" Cassius demands sharply. "You need to rest."

Della and Lawrence stand unmoving near the fire, but their silence weighs heavy in the air.

Remembering what Alaric said in the dream, I tuck the wrapped vial inside the bag, then stand.

I shake my head. "The coronation is sooner than we thought. We can't afford to waste any more time."

"Don't be foolish," he snaps. His fingers clamp around my upper arms and I halfway expect him to shake me. Instead, his eyes drift down to my chest as if he can see the pink scar through my shirt. "You were unconscious for days, nearly dead. That is not wasted time." Cassius lets go.

I press my palm to his chest and pull in a slow breath. It's unfair for me to be so angry with him.

He turns his pleading green eyes on me.

"While I still don't know exactly what you did to save me, I do appreciate it," I say. "But I've already lost too much time—I need to get back to him."

He presses a hand over mine, then says, "All right."

The two of us will need to talk at some point but now is not the time. Even though countless questions circle my thoughts, this is a conversation we should have in private.

After we all finish getting ready in silence, Cassius and I move toward the door, Ophelia's long, boney fingers brush over my shoulder. "You will need to head due west."

Cassius shakes his head. "We must travel south to Gloamfarrow for steeds and sustenance."

The oracle tsks at him like he's a child. "There will be horses awaiting you where the forest ends. They will have the provisions you need."

He narrows his eyes with suspicion, but she doesn't waver under his doubt. Finally, he says, "In that case, thank you."

"Speak no more of it, and may the saints of the Otherworld guide you."

Cassius nods and ducks out the door.

"Mr. Harkstead," Ophelia says.

I turn in time to see his back stiffen at the sharp tone of her voice. He stops in his tracks, then slowly turns and walks back to her. Bending at the waist, Lawrence lowers his ear to her mouth. She whispers, and his eyes widen at her words. His stony expression softens to pain before morphing into a mixture of relief and sorrow.

He strides past me without a glance, then speeds to the edge of the clearing, where he waits with his back to us.

Della smiles strangely at me, hanging back. It's clear she wants to speak to the oracle as well, so I follow after the two men, closing the door behind me.

Cassius cants his head to the side questioningly, though I have no answer to give him.

We don't have to wait long, and when Della emerges moments later, she is silent, her features adopting the emotionless mask most vampires favor. Then together, we set out toward Nightwich.

CHAPTER TWENTY-ONE

CLARA

We walk for hours toward the mountains. The forest gradually changes as we leave the magic behind. The air holds with the harsh bite of winter, and the spaces between trees feel natural. Branches and roots no longer tangle together, vying for the same space under the oracle's spell.

Della lags a fair distance behind, head bowed. Neither man seems to notice. I slow my pace until I'm walking beside her. It doesn't take much to figure out what's bothering her.

"What did she tell you?" I ask in a quiet whisper.

Della clenches her jaw as she lifts her head a fraction. Her eyes bore into Lawrence's back. "Nothing useful," she says hoarsely. "Mostly words that are meant to sound wise, about not being able to force the blind to see what they can't see." Then she turns her head down and away, ending our brief conversation.

There's no use pushing her to talk about it when she's not ready to.

"We should stop for a while and rest," Cassius announces.

Lawrence murmurs his agreement. I narrow my eyes and continue walking.

"Clara…" Cassius says.

The tone of his voice makes me stop.

Rounding on him, I jab his chest with a finger. "The three of you have been trying to get me to stop every hour." Taking a calming breath, I push down my irritation and then add, "I can keep going for now, so your concern is unnecessary."

All three vampires exchange glances as if I'm a wild demon, and they aren't sure how to handle me.

Cassius holds his hands up. "I understand," he says slowly. "But will you humor me and rest while we feed?"

Demon shit.

I hadn't thought about them needing blood before we reached the horses… selfishly, I hadn't thought of them at all.

The pressure of time presses down on my shoulders. There's only one thing to do. Compared to what I went through to get the potion from the oracle, this is a small price to pay.

Extending my arm, I say, "Then feed."

Lawrence's mouth drops open before he snaps it shut. His lips curl into an amused smile. Cassius grabs my arms and forces it back down with a glare.

Della snorts. "You were unconscious for six days. Do you think we went without food that whole time?"

"Thank you for the offer, but you need to keep your strength up," Cassius says, removing a flint from his jacket pocket.

They each pull a waterskin from their packs and sip while I chew on a stale piece of teek. It takes several large gulps of water to combat the effects of a few small bites. I can't afford to drink too much, so I stuff the remaining cake back into my pocket.

While I wait for my companions, I dig through my bag and pull out the vial, holding it up between my thumb and forefinger. Waning light pierces the deep blue liquid. It sparkles as it swishes back and forth— the same shade as Alaric's eyes. I scoff at the sentimental thought. It's so unlike me... or it was until I met him.

Clutching the vial, I shove it into my pocket, wanting to keep it close. There is so much left unsaid between us. Regret swells in my chest for the simple words I should have said when I had the chance, even if it was a death dream—I should have forced him to listen.

Leaning back against the tree, I stretch my legs out, crossing them at the ankles. Listening to the soft murmur of their conversation, my eyes grow heavier and heavier.

No, I can't stop to sleep yet.

I get up and move to stand in front of the fire and hold my hands over the flames to warm my chilled fingers. If I sit again, I'm afraid we'll end up staying here for the night, and we still have hours before the sun sets.

The moment Lawrence puts his waterskin into his pack, I kick dirt onto the fire, extinguishing it. No one says a word, but their expressions make their multitude of thoughts clear.

It's another two hours of walking before we reach the edge of the forest. As promised, three horses wait with full saddlebags. Della and Lawrence mount up and ride to the start of the trail that will take us through the mountains.

Cassius settles into the saddle on ours, then extends a hand to pull me up behind him. Taking up the reins in one hand, he rests the other on my knee.

I stiffen. We rode together on the way here. But being pressed up against him like this, now that we're tied, feels too intimate.

Cassius frowns over his shoulder. "Do not act so glum, little bird. It is not about your lack of skill," he says, misinterpreting my demeanor. "Despite what you wish to believe, you are not back to your full strength yet. I would feel better having you ride with me, than risk having you fall and hit your head."

He reaches back for my hands and brings them around his waist. Reluctantly, I cling to him.

"Then let's go," I say.

There will be time later to talk about the magic that ties us together and how to break it.

He urges the horse into a trot, past the others, and leads the way up the narrow mountain pass. I rest my head against his back and close my eyes.

While the path is etched into the side of one mountain peak, never taking us too high, it *is* narrow and steep enough to kill a falling human with the sharp rocks protruding from the slope.

The valley yawns out in front of us as we crest the final stretch. From here, we will descend from the mountains, then ride straight across the plains to Nightwich.

My fingers ache from my death grip on Cassius. I squint, trying to make out the details of the castle in the distance, but my human eyes are not good enough as the sun dips below the horizon bathing the world in shadow.

"Ease up, little bird, or I fear you will squeeze the life out of me yet," Cassius murmurs with a laugh.

I startle and release him, sliding my hands to rest on my knees just as he pulls the horse to a stop at an outcropping.

"We need to give the horses rest," he says, dismounting with far too much grace. He turns to offer me a hand, but I'm already sliding inelegantly down. "And you, Clara."

Stopping for even a moment makes my chest tighten. But he hasn't suggested another after our initial break in the forest. He isn't insisting on this to frustrate me or make Alaric suffer. Getting back to Nightwich in time will be pointless if I destroy myself or others in the process.

"You're right," I say without a fight.

His head draws back, brows raising. "And here I was preparing myself for a fight."

I snort and take a few steps before looking back over my shoulder. "It's not a compromise if only one of us gives in, is it?"

Lawrence and Cassius set to work feeding and stripping the tack from the horses, then brushing them down. Della and I gather small woody plants growing from cracks in the rock, piling them in the center of camp.

I struggle to get the wood to light before I

remember the flint. Turning to ask Cassius if I can borrow the tool, my nose bumps against his knee. He steps back, and I crane my neck to look up at him.

Cassius extends the flint with a smug look. "I was wondering when you would ask for this."

I pluck it from his hand and offer a matching, playfully sardonic smile. "I didn't."

His mouth drops open, realizing he spoke too soon. I turn away to focus on the fire, ignoring the way heat prickles up my neck to my face. It takes several attempts before a flame catches.

I lift my hand without looking and offer to return the flint. Rather than taking it, Cassius pats my head and says, "Keep it for now."

Dropping to the ground, I cross my legs and heave a sigh.

"What is that about?" Della asks. Her full lips pull into a knowing smile.

"What business is it of yours?" I bite out. It seems her unwillingness to open up to me earlier bothers me more than I realized.

She sucks in a sharp breath, her back straightening. "You should get some sleep if you want to leave as soon as possible," she says flatly.

I get to my feet and dust myself off before making my way to one of the two bedrolls lying side by side near the sheer wall of rock. Sleeping in shifts makes sense, but I doubt any of them will wake me for my turn.

Irritated, I climb onto the one set against the rock wall and turn my back on everyone, clutching my arms to my chest. Cassius lays down beside me as I settle in.

I do my best to let my annoyance go, knowing I'm the cause of my own foul mood, and try to sleep.

It feels as if only minutes have passed, and beneath the night sky, it's impossible to tell. The space at my back is empty and cold. I sit up, rubbing sleep from my eyes and looking for whatever woke me.

My vampire companions huddle around the fire. They must have added to it because the flames are considerably higher now.

"Something is coming," Della hisses from the far side of the fire.

"What is it?" Lawrence demands a little louder.

"I don't know." She lifts her head and looks off into the distance.

That has my attention.

Pointing to the sky, she says, "There's something

in that direction buzzing. I only followed it for a few miles before coming back."

Climbing to my feet, I squint in the direction she's pointing but I only see the stars twinkling against the dark sky.

"There," she says. "That black cloud. See how it moves? It's not natural."

"Let's not stick around to find out what it is. The two of you prepare the horses," Cassius orders.

Inching closer to the edge of the trail and away from the fire, my eyes strain to see what they do.

Cassius appears in front of me in a blink, grasping my shoulders. The air swirls wisps of hair around my face from his speed.

"Are you ready to go?" he asks, glancing over his shoulder.

I nod. "What is it?"

He only shakes his head and leads me to the horses, not bothering to repack the bedrolls. My head buzzes with fear.

No... The constant droning is coming from all directions. I look over my shoulder as he drags me behind him. One by one, the stars are blotted out by a large, dark mass.

When my feet stop, Cassius tugs on me again, then snakes am arm around my waist to lift me onto the horse.

The buzzing turns into a strange noise, a mix between a chirp and a short succession of screeches. Something swoops past my head with powerful wings. It's gone before I catch sight of it.

We race down the mountain pass as quickly as we can. I turn to glance back at our hastily abandoned camp. My breath catches in my throat.

One of the creatures glides close to the fire. Large leathery wings on a bird-like body flap erratically, trying to change direction. The long narrow beak opens with a shriek, displaying rows of razor-sharp teeth.

Another collides with the first, sending them crashing to the ground. The others flock around the two fallen creatures, and attack.

Seconds later, they fly away, leaving nothing but bones where the two fell.

The reason no one has ever returned from the pass was not because it was a labyrinth of paths, but because they fell prey to these creatures.

CHAPTER TWENTY-TWO

CLARA

"We can't run the horses, or we'll risk one breaking a leg!" Cassius shouts over the thundering hooves and maddening drone.

"There's no other choice," Lawrence calls back.

Screeching and buzzing follow as we descend the last leg of the mountain pass.

The sky gradually lightens at our backs. The swarm stands out, dark and ominous against the fading blue as it turns blood red from the dawning sun.

"What are those things?" I gasp.

"Nothing good," Cassius responds. He urges the horse faster, but the path wends as we near the plains.

"We can't outrun them for long," Lawrence says.

We need shelter, but there is nothing except the

narrow road ahead. I shudder. We'll be nothing more than a pile of bones in seconds once they reach us. With their inhuman speed and strength, the vampires could probably get away easily if it weren't for me. My humanity is slowing us down.

There has to be something we can do.

The flesh-eating birds blot out the rising light as they gain.

"Run the horses," I shout into the wind.

Lawrence doesn't hesitate, and Della follows closely on his heels. Cassius looks over his shoulder and frowns, shaking his head.

"I have an idea, but we need to gain some ground before we stop," I explain.

"Stop?" Cassius shouts. "That's insane!"

"I have an idea."

"How?"

I tighten my hold. "Get us a few minutes ahead of them if you can."

Cassius pushes our horse to go as fast as it can. The animal slides and leaps along the uneven path. Each precarious step is bone jarring.

I reach back with one hand and fish around in a saddle bag. The horse stumbles slightly, and I let out a strangled cry.

"Keep going!" I shout, still searching.

Then my fingers brush against the thick, worn

parchment of the map. I yank it out and hold it between my teeth. bite down on it, keeping both hands free.

It seems like a lifetime passes before we reach the plains. My palms grow damp. I pull in a breath and blow it out, trying to calm my pulse. No good will come from letting my nerves get to me and fumbling around.

The horses double their speed once we reach flat ground. Minutes pass as I wait for Cassius to stop, but we continue the punishing pace. The horse's breathing is labored, and sweat slicks its neck. I squeeze Cassius.

"Are you sure?" he calls out.

"Trust me," I say around the map and hope my hunch is correct.

Cassius urges the horse faster. I'm about to protest when he jerks us to a sudden stop.

I slide down and pull the flint from my pocket as I kneel. Using my knees to hold the map, I strike the flint. A small spark flies but doesn't catch.

"What in the Otherworld are you two doing?" Lawrence yells, circling his horse around us. "Are you insane?"

Cassius dismounts. "Gather moss and anything flammable!" he shouts. The horse dances and skitters in place, wanting to run from the swarm.

Beads of sweat trickle down my spine as I try again. A breeze picks up. I twist and curl my body around the map.

"Whatever you're doing, you might want to hurry before those things make a meal of us all," Lawrence growls.

The first creature swoops past, scraping my cheek with the tip of a wing. It stings. I ignore the trickle of blood trailing down my face. Two more scream, angling toward me.

Cassius reaches me in time to swat the first away, then the other, as its talons rake through my hair. He stays at my side, protecting me as more and more catch up.

I fumble with the flint, nearly dropping it.

Slow down, Clara. Stay calm...

I take a deep breath then try again. A pile of twigs and dried debris drop at my side. I snatch up a chunk of moss and stuff it into the center of the rolled map. Then I strike the flint again.

"We are going to die," Della says. The note of her voice filled with disbelief and surprise rather than horror.

A spark catches on the moss, burning long enough to spread to the map. I quickly wrap a handful of twigs around it with a fistful of moss in the center. Cassius grabs my elbow, helping me stand.

Raising my arm, the swarm changes directions. The flames swoosh and sway with the wind of their beating wings. I step around Cassius and shove the makeshift torch into their path. They scatter to avoid the fire.

Understanding, the two men take the sticks at my feet and hold them into my flame until they catch.

I arc my arm through the air, extending the radius as much as possible.

We circle in front of Della, struggling to keep the horses from bolting as the swarm catches up. Wings slice my arms and legs with each pass.

This won't last. I grit my teeth as the fire inches lower. Doubt invades my thoughts, conquering the thin shred of hope I had.

The fire burns closer and closer to my hand, singeing my skin. Leathery wings beat the air with sharp edges, slicing and cutting our flesh when one manages to slip through our defenses.

I hold on, only releasing the map when I have no choice. The skin on the top of my hand is raw and blistered.

A hand clamps around the back of my neck, then forces me to my knees. The swarm continues to thin out until only a few remain. Cassius waves his makeshift torch of sticks wildly in the air. Then with a curse, he lets it drop as it runs out.

Drawing the dagger, I ignore the pain from my burned hand brushing against my sleeve. I jump to my feet and slice across the body of a bird beast soaring overhead, toward Cassius's blind spot. It crumples in the air, then skids and tumbles along the ground.

Beams of light stretch across the plains through the clear morning sky just as Lawrence's torch runs out.

Screeching fills the air, joining the thunder of wildly beating wings. The remaining beasts retreat back toward the mountains.

I collapse to all fours, panting. My clothing is cut along my arms and legs, but we're alive. The thick material saved me from worse injury.

Black riding boots stop in front of me. I sit back on my haunches, balling my hands into fists to keep them from trembling.

"How did you know that would work?" Lawrence asks.

"I wasn't entirely sure," I say honestly. "At the camp, they seemed to be blinded or confused by the fire…" I trail off, not sure what else to say.

The corner of his mouth quirks up, and then he laughs—a full belly laugh—holding his stomach as he bends at the waist.

Cassius takes my elbow and helps me rise to my

feet. I ignore him as he checks me over for injuries. Della bumps my shoulder and gives me a questioning glance, frowning at her sire. I shrug and shake my head. Eventually, Lawrence's laughter dies down, and he swipes at his face.

"Care to share what is so amusing with the rest of us?" Cassius asks dryly.

I roll my eyes. Lawrence sweeps me up in an embrace, pinning my arms to my side as spins me around.

"Do you two realize what happened?" He sets me down, eyes sparkling with amusement. "A human just saved our vampire asses because she was the only one who observed those creatures." He breaks out in more laughter.

Cassius pulls me into his side by the back of my neck and kisses the top of my head. "That she did."

I duck from between them and move to Della's far side. She seems to be less likely to embrace me.

These demon sent vampires are so affectionate.

Feeling uncomfortable, I shrug it off. "I am used to things trying to kill me," I say waving to indicate the three of them. "The rest of you are used to being the predators, not the prey."

"What were those things anyway?" Della asks. "I've never heard of such a creature."

Cassius turns to check the horses and says, "In all

my years, I have heard of no legends that describe anything like that. My best guess is that it's a mutation caused by the extra power leaking from the Otherworld, or demons mating with various flying creatures. There are many peculiar things in this area."

Della shudders.

"It's getting late," I say. We have another full day's ride ahead of us at the very least.

They murmur their agreements, and we all mount up and ride, keeping the pace. It's slow, but at least we are moving.

An hour after the sun sets, a city of lights glitters on the horizon. I sit up straight and lean forward. Cassius wraps an arm around my middle and pulls me back.

"Don't fly away just yet, little bird. We still have a long way to go." He pulls the horse to a stop.

I twist to face him. "We're almost there."

"It's not as close as you think," he explains, dismounting and helping me down. "We'll rest here for a few hours."

Lawrence and Della say nothing as they obey.

Nightwich is on the horizon and I can't tear my eyes from the city. The pressure of time grows heavier with each passing minute. We are so close, I can practically taste it.

Cassius walks up behind me and takes my shoulders, turning me away from Alaric and toward the fire. "We can't have you exhausted when we return. You need to keep a level head now more than ever."

Nodding, I let him steer me toward the fire.

Even knowing it's only my imagination, I can almost feel Alaric's presence through the mark.

CHAPTER TWENTY-THREE

CLARA

I pace at the edge of camp, unable to tear my gaze from the castle set against the black wall of mountains. The crescent-shaped city rings Nightwich, glittering like the cloudless starry sky above. It's beautiful from this distance, as if it belongs in a fairytale.

After we made camp and ate, I managed to rest for a few hours before my frantically beating heart woke me. The nightmare of returning to Nightwich only to find Alaric oath bound to Elizabeth kept me from going back to sleep.

Cassius clears his throat when my feet take me just outside the ring of firelight. Not venturing any further, I plant my feet but don't return to the fire. I can't sit around and relax. He fears her and not just for his loss of freedom. There's more to it than that.

Who would have ever thought I would be so desperate to save a vampire? I shake my head. Even now, after everything I've been through with Alaric and for him, there are moments I still have trouble wrapping my mind around that.

"Here," Della says, flipping the fur-lined hood over my head. She stands next to me with her arms crossed under her chest and hip jutting out. "It's cold tonight."

"Mmm," I say noncommittally.

"You're not as boring as I thought you were," she says with a lilt, as if it's a compliment.

I snort, running my hands up and down my arms.

"I mean it. You're not the scared little human girl I thought you were when we first arrived at Windbury." Della laughs to herself. "We all thought Alaric had gone mad when we realized *you* were the human he claimed. The scent of fear clung to you the second you walked in, so we didn't expect you to live much longer..." She trails off.

I glare at her from the corner of my eye. Wisps of fur from my hood blur her profile. Della is entirely serious and I'm not sure if I should be insulted or not.

"You're more determined than most vampires I know... and that makes you powerful," she says.

Giving up trying to ignore her, I swivel my head to

meet her gaze. Dark eyes scan me with a look one might dare to call admiration.

Della is not the same vampire who confided in me that she loved her sire in her strangely clinical way. Nothing like the self-important woman, insulted when I refused to kiss her hand in greeting. She's softened by sorrow and pain no weapon can deliver.

"What did you talk to the oracle about?" I ask, glancing back at the two men chatting quietly among themselves.

Della follows my gaze. "I think you already know the answer."

Guilt leaves a sour taste on my tongue. I do know. Some part of me has known since she stepped foot out of that cabin. The pain in her eyes when she looks at Lawrence is telling. She is in love with a man who is still in love with another woman. "I—"

"It's all right. I never expected anything," Della cuts me off, but her words ring false.

The longing in her voice… I understand. "But you had to try?"

She nods. I reach my hand into my pocket and clutch the vial. Nothing about being with Alaric has been easy. Love isn't easy, but it is worth fighting for.

"She said, 'What is meant to be will be.'"

"That isn't particularly helpful."

Della hums in agreement then says, "Though, in a

strange way, I think that it's exactly what I needed to hear." She turns her dark eyes on me. They shine, thick with unshed tears. "I no longer have to hold on to hope. Perhaps now, I can finally let go."

My heart aches for her. Hope is no small thing to abandon, but sometimes it is necessary to do so if you wish to survive.

The sound of hooves approaching silences our conversation.

"Since you refuse to sleep anymore, we will set out." Cassius hands a set of reins to Della then leaps onto our horse, reaching his hand down to help me up. "We'll be in the city by the time the sun sets."

My fingers curl into my palms and I snatch my hand back, holding it to my chest as if he tried to bite me. "The city?"

His grip tightens on the leather reins. "I know you are anxious, little bird, but we cannot show up at the castle in this state."

Gritting my teeth, I glare up at him, ignoring his outstretched hand. The kindness of his expression falls into neutrality.

"You are being impulsive again," he points out. "Elizabeth believes I was dealing with matters at my personal manor, bringing my soon-to-be oath bonded with me, with Della and Lawrence serving as chaperons. If we show up looking as if we traveled halfway across the world, it would be suspicious."

Cassius is right. Everything he says makes sense, but after what I've been through—what we've all been through—I find it almost impossible to have patience when we're so close.

Slipping my hand into his, I let him lift me into the saddle.

My arms go around his waist and I press my cheek to his back. "I'm sorry, I don't know why I haven't been able to think straight."

He lays a hand over mine, then guides the horse forward. "The heart has a way of overriding the brain. It is an unfortunate side effect of being in love. Especially when they are suffering or in danger."

I've been thinking about this all wrong. How many years had I spent perched in a tree waiting for some small animal to wander by? How many times did I keep trying when my arrow missed, until I was able to catch something for that night's stew?

This isn't so different. I will wait for my moment and make my move when the time is right.

As much as it pains me to see Alaric under Elizabeth's control, I must tread carefully.

"The moon is nearly full," Lawrence remarks, bringing his horse up alongside ours. The strange comment pulls me from my thoughts.

"In three nights," Cassius agrees. "That is a good sign."

"Yes," I say dryly. "It's been so long since I've seen one… at least a month."

Lawrence snorts. "How you can be involved with vampires and know so little is beyond me."

Before I can offer a scathing retort, Cassius interjects, "With the coronation coming up, the queen will throw a Red Hunt."

The name alone sends a chill down my spine. "What is that?" I ask, not sure I want to know any details.

"On the first night of a full moon preceding an event, Elizabeth takes the ladies of her court and leads them in a hunt from sunset to sunrise," Cassius says.

Lawrence draws up level with me. "I'm sure you can figure out where the Red Hunt got its name."

"The city won't expect another one so soon after the solstice," Della remarks from Lawrence's other side.

"It is unfortunate for them," Cassius murmurs. "However, it will provide us with the opportunity we need."

My hold on him tightens.

The sun rises an hour into our ride, gilding the castle. As we near the edge of town, I hold my breath in an attempt to rein in my excitement.

"Calm," Cassius says as if he can read my mind. "We are almost there."

Skirting the city, we enter from one of the many side roads and stick to the outer edge. After a while, angle in toward one of the impressive manors clustered in the area.

We enter through the wrought iron gates of the manor and are greeted by a butler. He takes the reins while we dismount, then leads the horse away without a word. Della and Lawrence agree to meet us back here in three hours then leave to feed properly.

Cassius slips his hand into mine and leads me through the halls. I gape at the ostentatious interior. Yards and yards of fabric cover the windows in shades of white and gold. The floors are dark, polished hardwood with thick carpet runer that I sink into with every step. And there isn't a single wall without a stunning piece of art.

Passing the drawing room, I crane my neck to

peek inside. With so much furniture crammed inside the room, there's little space left to navigate.

Cassius continues to guide me through the halls and up to the second floor. Thick material winds around the banister of the stairs. Not an inch of this place is undecorated or plain. Even the molding has intricate designs carved into the wood.

It isn't until we enter a masculine bedroom decorated with dark wood and rich green fabrics with silver accents, that I even think to question where he's taking me.

"Why are we in your bedroom?" I cringe inwardly at the high pitch of my voice.

Cassius releases my hand and strides across the room to a door on the far side. He jerks his head, motioning for me to go in. "Bathe and I will return shortly. Help yourself to whatever you need."

Half an hour later, bubbles slowly leak from my mouth, then all at once as I empty my lungs. I break the surface of the water, gasping for air, and lean back against the side of the tub, pushing my hair off my face.

The hot water feels good on my sore muscles. It would be easy to fall asleep if I didn't think Cassius might barge through the door if I take too long.

Grabbing the towel beside the tub, I quickly dry off before wrapping myself and wringing the excess water from my hair. I pad over to the door and open it just wide enough to peek out. Cool air rushes in, sending goosebumps racing along my skin.

"Cassius?" I call out.

No answer.

Despite the expensive furnishings and the large fire blazing in the bedroom's hearth. The manor feels hollow… like he's never truly lived here. It's unsettling in a way that rivals being in a room full of hungry vampires. Feeling strangely exposed, I shiver and close the door.

Clutching the towel tighter, I sit on the edge of the tub. The air slowly cools as I wait, but I don't want to put the dirty clothes back on. Several minutes pass with only my breathing for company. Then I catch the distant sound of the front door opening, and then closing.

There's a soft knock, and when I don't answer, Cassius calls to me through the door. "Clara?"

Feeling foolish for acting like it could have been anyone else, I turn the knob and pull it open.

Cassius frowns. His face looks fuller, and the color that leached from his skin has returned to his cheeks. I hadn't realized how pale and gaunt his face became on the journey.

"These are for you," he says, shoving a bundle into my arms.

Scrambling to take the clothing without dropping the towel, I mutter, "Thank you."

Cassius waves a hand and turns away. "It's nothing."

"No," I say firmly, reaching out for his arm. He stops in his tracks and faces me as if compelled to do so. "I mean for everything." I shake my head and swallow. "I've been so caught up in my mission, that I didn't see how much the three of you sacrificed to help me."

"Say no more." He waves a hand and begins to turn away.

Stepping into the room, I block his path. "Lawrence is his friend, but you hate him," I push.

Cassius presses his lips into a thin line. His unfocused eyes stare through the dancing flames. "It's true that I hold no fondness for him. Alaric has always had everything I've ever wanted and rejected it at every turn." His shoulders slump as he drags his gaze to meet mine. "Even I can see Elizabeth's actions are wrong." He brushes a damp lock of hair away from my face. "But I didn't do any of this for him, little bird. I did it for you."

"Cassius…"

He steps in closer and cradles my face in his hands. "I am your friend, Clara. I will always be your friend."

"Why?" I ask breathlessly. I shouldn't push the issue. But I don't understand why he would tie his life to mine just because he cares for me... especially when he knows my heart belongs to Alaric.

"You are a frustrating creature, constantly throwing yourself into situations without thought. How could any vampire resist that?" He smirks.

With a frustrated sigh, I step back. I want real reasons from him, to understand his motivation, not whatever this façade is where he tries to be charming and use my negative attributes as a distraction.

Cassius leans in and places a kiss on my forehead then a soft, chaste kiss on my mouth.

"We should all be so lucky to have the love of someone willing to go to the Otherworld and back for us." He smiles and pulls away. "I know you will never be mine, little bird, and I have made my peace with that but know that I will always be here if you need someone to turn to or a place to go."

I nod, my throat too tight to speak, even if I wasn't already lost for words.

Cassius guides me back by the shoulders until I'm in the bathing room then closes the door between us.

Quickly dressing, I try to get my brain to restart. I need to distance myself from him. While I have come to think of him as a friend, it doesn't feel right to accept his help as I have when I will never return his feelings.

I reenter the room and Cassius has me sit in a chair before the fire and brushes the knots out with his hands as the warmth dries the strands.

Every time I want to ask how we are tied, my mouth goes dry, and my tongue feels heavy and clumsy. I should know, but I can't bring myself to ask just yet. Curling my legs up, I close my eyes and relax into the feeling of his fingers running through my hair.

A hand tightens around my shoulder giving me a gentle shake. Blinking up at Cassius, I rub my hands over my face wondering when I fell asleep.

"The others are waiting out front with fresh horses," he says.

Cassius loops my arm through his. I try to pull back. A crooked grin spreads over his face as he pins me to his side as we walk out of the front door.

Both Lawrence and Della look refreshed as well. Their faces are no longer sallow from the journey but full and healthy. Somehow, I will have to find a way to repay them all for everything they've done.

Before I can utter a word, Della motions for us to hurry.

Cassius settles himself in the saddle and reaches

down to offer me his hand one more time, pulling me up in front of him. Then we ride out of the gates and toward the castle.

CHAPTER TWENTY-FOUR

CLARA

My pulse leaps into my throat as we draw closer to the castle.

"Do not underestimate the queen's compulsion over Alaric. He is powerful, but his power pales in comparison to hers," Cassius warns.

I dip my chin.

The horse comes to a stop just outside the stables and dismounts. Issuing a farewell to Cassius, Della, and Lawrence go their separate ways, not even glancing my way.

"Remember, you are a well-behaved human. *My human*," he whispers in my ear.

Again, I lower my chin imperceptibly in acknowledgment.

"Do nothing to draw attention to yourself."

I pull in a sharp breath. *Is that even possible?*

He cups the back of my neck and presses his cheek to mine, nuzzling his nose near my ear. "If she suspects, then you will not live to see him free."

Cassius straightens and walks out of the stables as I follow a step behind with my head bowed. There are at least a dozen vampires in the main hall when we enter. Their eyes bore into us—into me.

Snickering and whispers reach my ears. They're pleased that their prince had his claimed and marked human given to another after spurning their ways for so long. Outside, I'm poised, my face placid and void of all emotion. Inside, I seethe from their petty jealousy.

Unlike Elizabeth, these vampires are easy to fool. All I have to do is drop my eyes, and they believe I have been cowed into being a meek human.

Cassius wraps an arm around my waist, bringing his head down to the spot below my ear, and nips. I gasp and barely keep from driving my elbow into his ribs.

"Have patience, little bird. It won't be much longer now," he whispers.

Understanding his unspoken words, I remain silent and keep my head down. I won't be able to relax until my plan has succeeded.

The clock tower chimes, signaling an hour before sunset.

I pace, needing to release my excess energy. Getting the potion took nearly two weeks, and now two more days have slipped through my fingers. This wait will be the death of me.

Even after promising Cassius that I wouldn't act prematurely, he hasn't let me step foot outside this room without him, Lawrence, or Della by my side.

Tonight is the night.

For the millionth time today, I check that my dagger is securely strapped to my arm and the vial is in my pocket. My fingers itch to put things into motion.

The sound of horses outside draws me to the window. I press my face against the glass to catch a glimpse, hoping it's Elizabeth finally leaving the castle grounds.

No such luck. My room is not at an angle to see anything.

Giving up, I flop down on the rickety bed. A plume of dust billows into the air. Just as I close my eyes, the door opens. I'm on my feet in a second, hand reaching for the dagger and heart thundering in my throat.

Della frowns, closing the door behind her. She holds a small, amber glass jar in her hand, half-wrapped in a white cloth.

It's time.

"What is the plan?" I ask, meeting her in the middle.

She removes the lid and dips part of the rag into the clear salve without answering. "Tilt your head," she orders.

Della smears the cold salve down the side of my neck and shoulder, then motions for me to tilt it the other way, repeating the process.

"Now your wrists," she says.

I hold out my arms for her. She pushes up my sleeve and smears more of it from my wrists to my inner elbow. The scent is sweet with subtle floral notes.

"What is this?" I ask.

Pausing in her work, Della looks up and smiles. "Nightshade."

I don't move for several seconds while I wrap my mind around that word. Where she placed the salve are key points. "Isn't that poisonous?"

"Not to vampires." She winks. "It's only a sedative for us."

"What about to humans?" I ask, concerned.

Della waves me off. "You don't plan on licking those spots, do you?" When I shake my head, she says, "Then you'll be fine. Since we won't be there to help you, it's our insurance that you'll most likely make it out alive."

"What do I need to do?" I ask again. Then the meaning of her words snags my full attention. "Wait —*most likely?*"

The clear substance dries quickly on my skin until it's impossible to tell it was ever there.

"Go to the training room," she says, putting the lid back on the jar and sealing it tight.

I blink. "Training?"

"Just be yourself and this will work. Now go, and hurry." She half-pushes me out of the door.

I run from the room down to the lower level, avoiding the busy halls, and decide on using the servant's quarters.

I might not know what the three of them are up to, but judging from the places Della smeared the nightshade, it seems that my part is to be vampire bait.

The hall is deathly silent and dark. Tonight, there's only one torch lit at the far end. Staying quiet, I make my way to the training room and push open the door. All but two torches were recently extinguished bathing the room in shadow. The acrid scent of their smoke still lingers.

"Hello?" I call out. My voice echoes around the chamber, but no one answers.

Stopping in the center of the room, I pull my dagger from the sheath and wait. The metal blade glints in the firelight, making it appear almost molten. Alaric's words from the night he gave it to me reverberate through my memory.

"Because I want to see how sweet that sharp tongue of yours tastes. And because I want you to mean it when you try to stab me through the heart with my own weapon."

I shiver and hope it doesn't come down to that.

A gust of wind blows a strand of hair against my face and I barely have time to lift my head before Cassius wrenches my arm, forcing me to kneel. When my knees strike the stone with a jarring crack, he rips the dagger from my grasp.

Lowering his face to mine, his lips brush my ear as he whispers, "I am truly sorry for this, little bird."

Then the blade slides along my arm. Blood wells up, gushing from the deep cut. Uselessly, I try to press the wound closed with my other hand.

Cassius flings the dagger. Sparks light as the metal scrapes across the stone, sliding out into the dark hall.

"Now, do what you do best," he says. And then, he's gone.

A hiss escapes my lips as I look around. Taking a deep breath, I push to my feet. Dizziness washes over me and my shoulder slams into the wall. Bouncing off, I stumble forward falling to my hands and knees before the weapon.

Stars explode across my vision from the impact, and I whimper. Blood runs down my arm and coats the front of my shirt. I curse Cassius for cutting too deep.

My heart hammers against my chest. There's no way I can protect myself unless I wrap my arm. With my good hand, I bite the edge of my shirt between my teeth and hold it, angling the dagger to slice a length of material off.

I should wear longer shirts or start carrying bandages. Even though it's not funny, I nearly laugh. But that momentary lapse is short-lived by the stab of pain radiating along my arm as I struggle to wrap it.

"Lawrence," Alaric's husky voice calls from the foot of the stairs.

I raise my head and meet his steely gaze.

No. I'm not ready.

It feels like an eternity as we take each other in. Then in the span of a heartbeat, Alaric lifts off the ground and slams me hard against the wall. He watches me with a cold, unfamiliar expression as I claw uselessly at his wrist with one hand.

Slowly, Alaric lowers me but keeps his hand around my throat.

"Please," I gasp.

This is his face, but the Alaric I know is not there behind the familiar sapphire eyes ringed with violent, glowing red. His upper lip curls with pure hate.

Frustration, pain, and desperation burn the backs of my eyes until everything is a blur. One blink and heavy tears slide down my cheeks as Alaric looks on in rapt interest.

Abruptly, his hand loosens, sliding down my neck, and taking hold of the front of my shirt, he drags me into the training room, throwing me to the floor. I fall awkwardly, curling into myself to protect my injured arm. The door slams with a resounding crack.

Alaric stalks toward me with slow, deliberate steps. I struggle to stand on unsteady legs. Spots form, dancing and blotting out parts of my vision.

How can I survive this if Alaric kills me with his bare hands? This was a terrible plan.

I back up until I bump into a wall. Trapped. Alaric closes the distance with blinding speed and tangles a hand in my hair, wrenching my neck to the side. The sharp movement rips the air from my lungs.

"Please… Alaric. I know you don't want to do this," I whimper.

The fingers of his other hand glide down the back

of my arm and entwine with my own. He brings my arm up and presses the back of my hand to the wall. Blood continues to flow in thick rivulets. His eyes glitter with fury and desire.

My entire body trembles, limbs turning ice cold before going numb.

Alaric watches the blood run down my arm as if hypnotized. Then slowly, he settles his face in the crook of my neck. His lips gently press against the patch of scarred skin for a long moment.

It almost feels as if he brushes the barest kiss against my throat a second before sinking his fangs in.

Expecting blinding pain and fire as he rips into my flesh, it surprises me how kind the bite is. Even with so much anger radiating from him and distorting his face, there is nothing beyond a small ache.

It's not his anger.

Alaric drinks, and with each pull of blood, my strength fades until I can no longer stand on my own. He holds me up, pinning me to the wall with his body.

A sob catches in my throat. *I was so close...*

Now, he'll never be free.

He draws back, searching my face. His pupils expand and contract. Confusion furrows his brow as the nightshade takes hold.

The rise and fall of his chest quickens with short breaths. Alaric sways as his eyes accuse me of betrayal. He stumbles. The heel of his boot catches on the uneven floor, sending him toppling back. He lands hard.

I fall to my knees at his side. Murder and rage distort his features, but none of it is his.

How cruel to force him to kill me with his own hand.

I shoulder him, throwing my weight into it, and roll him onto his back. I end up with my face pressed against his chest. My hands and arms are clumsy, refusing to obey. I can only imagine how we look—struggling and both unable to fight.

Clutching my injured arm to my chest, I straddle him as I reach into my pocket for the vial. Alaric growls, fighting against the effects of the nightshade.

"I'm sorry," I breathe, panting.

The red dims until it vanishes from his eyes, leaving his crystal blue depths clear and bright.

Using my teeth to pull the cork from the vial, I spit it out and lean forward. My hand shakes as I press the brim to his mouth. Alaric wriggles underneath me, gaining strength—the nightshade won't last much longer.

I set my palm on the stone next to his head to steady myself.

His lips refuse to part. Lowering my face, I kiss the corner of his mouth, and whisper, *"Please."*

Alaric stops fighting just long enough for me to wedge the edge of the vial between his lips. I tilt the glass, pouring the syrupy liquid into his mouth, only a few drops manage to escape.

The empty vial slips from my hand and clatters to the floor. I cover his mouth and lean forward to keep him from spitting it out. Alaric's throat bobs as he swallows the potion.

The anger and rage slowly fade from his eyes. After a minute, I let my hand fall away.

"Alaric?" I breathe his name.

Other than the steady rise and fall of his chest against mine, he doesn't move. I roll off and lie on the cold stone floor next to him. Waiting and watching.

A single twitch of his shoulder sets off a chain reaction. Muscle spasms roll down his body, back arching and neck straining. I reach for him but am helpless to do anything in my state.

An eternity seems to pass before he goes still. Alaric's head lulls to face me. Then slowly, he brings his hand up toward my face. His knuckles brush against my cheek, and then his eyes slide closed.

There's no movement in his chest, and my own heart skips several beats.

"Alaric?" I say, but there's no response. "Alaric… Alaric?" My voice becomes shrill as panic sets in.

For a moment, the pain lancing its way up my arm is forgotten as I push myself up and shake him. When he doesn't respond, I bring my hand up, cringing, and slap his face. "You have to wake up!" I bite out. My vision blurs as fresh tears spring up.

His skin is cold to the touch.

Like death.

He can't be dead. He can't be.

The cracking inside my chest is deafening as I begin to shatter. What little hope I have manages to cling to slips through my fingers as the tether of Alaric's mark is stretched taut, then unravels.

No… no, no no! This isn't supposed to happen. I want to scream the words, but my lungs refuse to work.

The witch had promised… she promised—and it was a lie. It may have broken Elizabeth's hold, but it killed him.

With half-numb fingers, I clasp his hand and curl into his side. The last thread of the mark snaps, stealing the breath from my lungs. A shudder rolls through my body.

I open my mouth in a silent scream, unable to take the pain. It feels like my veins are being shredded as the last of Alaric's power rips free of me. I tighten my hold until the cold, bitter dark swallows me up.

CHAPTER TWENTY-FIVE

CLARA

Fiery pain slices through the dark, dragging me back from the brink of nothingness. I suck in a dry, painful gasp of air and open my eyes. Della glares intently at my arm, tying the last of the stitches.

"You idiot girl, you nearly let yourself be killed," she hisses.

Cassius cradles my head in his lap. "What happened?"

I turn my head toward Alaric's still form. Hot tears spill down my face as I choke back a sob. "It didn't work," I rasp through my burning throat.

Cassius helps me to my feet then guides me into Della's arms.

"Leave me—"

"You can't stay here, Clara," Cassius says.

"I don't care. I don't want to leave him."

Della stands, refusing to let go. My weak struggles are nothing against her vampire strength.

I don't care if Elizabeth finds me and kills me for murdering him. It's what I deserve.

"Take her to my room," Cassius orders. "I will clean up this mess before anyone discovers what took place."

Without another word, Della shifts so my good arm is around her neck. It's a losing battle. When I don't cooperate, she throws me over her shoulder.

"My room," I croak out in a voice so raw, I don't recognize it as mine.

"I don't think that's a good idea," she says.

"Please."

Della hesitates but changes course, speeding in the opposite direction and up the stairs to my sparse room. She settles me into the lumpy bed and begins to carefully remove my blood-soaked clothes. Della leaves my side. I remain sitting, staring at the dried blood along the edges of my fingernails.

A folded bundle lands in my hands. My heart stutters when she unfolds the large shirt. It's one of Alaric's.

With swift, efficient movements, Della cleans and wraps my wound, then covers me with the blanket when she's finished.

I shift onto my side, giving her my back. I bunch the collar and bring it to my nose, then inhale.

It still smells like him.

"I will return later to check on your cut." After a long silence, she adds, "I am truly sorry it turned out this way."

A moment later, the door clicks shut.

I promised Alaric I'd save him, then took his life instead. This is a horrible nightmare. Heat and tears combine, stinging my damp face like hot pinpricks. But the tears refuse to stop. I cry until there's nothing left but empty sobs and bone-deep grief. Still, the sleep I long for eludes my grasp.

An endless, aching pit resides in my chest where the mark used to reside. Its absence leaves me cold. Hollow. Squeezing my eyes shut, I reach out with my mind, calling to him, begging him to come back. But like the mark, he's gone.

I don't know how much time passes before exhaustion becomes too much, and I slip into unconsciousness.

"Clara," a familiar voice whispers, erasing fractured dreams.

I blink open my swollen eyes. Clouds cover the moon, bathing the room in utter darkness.

"Clara?" That deep, rich voice calls my name again.

I bolt up and drop my feet off the edge of the bed. My entire body aches with the sudden movement. Then a sliver of cold light finds its way past the clouds and spills through the window.

A distinctly masculine figure stands just behind the beam, then slowly steps forward. I bite down on the inside of my cheek and hold my breath, waiting for him to move forward into the light.

"Alaric?" My pulse drums in my ears. "I'm sorry…"

I stand and shuffle toward the specter of my dreams. He haunts me in death as he haunted me on the journey.

"Do not be sorry, my dear Clara." He stops a few feet in front of me. "You set me free."

I close the distance, tripping over myself, legs weak and uncoordinated. Alaric catches me around the waist as I crash into him.

Craning my neck, I lift my head and try to memorize every inch of his face. I don't know if he'll visit my dreams again. "You *died* because I failed."

A chuckle rumbles through his chest against my cheek as I inhale the masculine scent. I want to smack him for making light of this and kiss him senseless at the same time.

"Not quite," he says.

It takes entirely too long for me to understand what he means that I end up missing part of what he says next.

"…needed time to break the binds of Elizabeth's compulsion. I would have come to you earlier, but Cassius and Lawrence insisted on testing me before they would allow me anywhere near you." He kisses one eye and then the other. "But I assure you, I am very much alive."

A strangled sound, somewhere between a sob of pain and joy, works its way free. I slide my arms around his neck and bury my face against his chest. "I thought I lost you… I—I felt the mark break."

"Yes—"

I pull away and gather my hair over one shoulder, tilting my head to expose my neck. "Mark me again."

Alaric wraps his fingers around my wrist and kisses my palm. "As much as I would enjoy marking you all over again, you have lost far too much blood tonight and need to heal." His words are kind and filled with longing, but his features crumple with guilt. He waits several heartbeats before adding, "Elizabeth could very well kill you for breaking the compulsion."

"She doesn't frighten me." I snort derisively. "She has already tried."

"She will rip your heart from your chest," he adds in all seriousness as if I don't grasp the immensity of the situation.

But I do.

"I don't care. I would do it again a thousand times over if it means that you will be free. The oracle said you can never be compelled again but you're not protected from other magic."

Alaric tightens his arms around me and rests his head in the crook of my neck, inhaling deeply. We stay wrapped up in each other for a long moment. I revel in feeling him alive and in my arms for the first time in too long.

"I have missed you, my dear Clara," he whispers, sending goosebumps racing along my skin. When he finally pulls back, his eyes are filled with renewed pain. "I will still be oath bound to her in five weeks. And only death can break that bond..." He reaches up and runs his hands through my wild hair, smoothing it back. I can see him warring with his next words.

"I won't let that happen," I say before he can speak.

He shakes his head. "I will not have a choice. Her power far outweighs my own... She sired me."

Shrugging out of his embrace, I step back. "You do

have a choice." He starts to protest, but I continue, "Oath bind yourself to me."

Alaric shakes his head. "I cannot ask you to tie yourself to me for eternity."

"Why?"

"Because you deserve better," he says.

The anguish in his voice lights a fury deep inside me. *I will not let this go.*

I thrust my hands on my hips and shake my head. There is nothing better than him, *no one* better than him. "Then it's a good thing I'm the one who decides what I deserve, and what I want."

"You would be forced to live as long as I do, and you will never have the life you wanted, and that is only if Elizabeth doesn't find a way to punish you for it." Alaric offers nothing but excuses.

I press my fingers to his mouth to silence him. "I will not let her trap you again," I vow, then swallow the lump forming in my throat. "Unless you do not want to be bound to me?"

His features soften, the he presses his cheek to mine. "In all the years I have been *this*, I never thought I would want to be bound to anyone, until you, my dear Clara," he whispers. shifting, he brushes his lips over mine and mouths, *I love you.* "I do not want you to wake up one day, regretting it."

I clutch at his shirt and press a kiss along his jaw. "Do you have any idea what I've been through?"

Alaric pulls back to examine me, passing over my sliced arm as he looks for other injuries.

Reaching up, I tug the collar of my shirt down to expose the new pink scar on my chest. His eyes darken.

"I will risk everything to save you. I could never regret anything when it comes to you, Alaric Devereaux."

"What have you done?" He traces the fading pink line that will be fully healed in another few days. "How did you survive?"

I smooth the material back in place, not wanting to think about how. He needs to understand. "That doesn't matter right now."

A shiver rakes down my bones. I'm asking him to oath bind himself to me. I never expected to want something so permanent or meaningful. I don't want this purely for pragmatic reasons but because he holds my heart.

Forever with Alaric doesn't terrify me.

It feels right.

It should have crossed my mind before now that we would need to make this decision. Doing this will have repercussions, But I'm not afraid. I will meet those challenges head-on and fight for him... for us.

This vampire, who I once hated for what he was, has opened my eyes. He showed me what it meant to be a friend when I was alone, when it would have been easier to let me die on the grounds outside his manor. This vampire who was injured while saving my life, is willing to sacrifice his freedom to protect me. His very existence demands my loyalty and love.

He fought for me when no one else would… and stole my heart when I wasn't looking.

"I love you, Alaric," I whisper. "I have for a while, it just took me a long time to realize it."

For some reason, only the Otherworld knows why, my face burns with that admission. Never before have those three words held more truth when uttered.

"My heart… my life… they have always been yours." I used to think feeling that about someone would make me weak—now I realize it's the opposite.

He kisses me fiercely, crushing me to him. The movement is so sudden that I stumble back a few steps, bumping into the wall. He moves with me, unwilling to allow space between us.

"I have longed to hear you say those words. I will cherish them until the Otherworld takes me." He trails kisses down the column of my throat, pausing on the newly healed skin where he fed earlier. "But you don't need to do this… not after what I did to you."

"Look at me," I demand sharply.

He doesn't move.

"Look at me, Alaric," I say again.

Slowly, he raises his head.

"You are not responsible for what she compelled you to do." My hand slides along his jaw to the back of his neck and I pull him closer. "I want this because I cannot imagine a life without you. As long as you're by my side, I don't care what happens. I would want this even without her threats and plans. I want this… I want this because I love you, you fool of a vampire."

His shoulders sag with relief. Alaric reaches for my hand, bringing it to his lips, placing a kiss on my palm.

Then he drags a nail over that same spot, opening up a deep slice. It stings, but the sensation fades quickly. He repeats the process on his own hand and slides his fingers through mine. Lining up the cuts, he tightens his hold, letting our blood mingle.

It's not long before I can feel something happening. A light tingle at our clasped hands spreads through my veins with each pulsing of our hearts.

My eyes slide shut as a shiver runs down my spine. There is an intimacy in the way the connection slips into place, creating something tethering us together that is so much stronger than the mark. Alaric's power wends its way through my veins and around my heart, and I can sense him in a way I never thought possible.

Red power swallows Alaric's eyes as he lowers his face to mine. With my back against the wall, there's nowhere for me to go, but I don't want to be anywhere else.

My heart pounds loudly against my ribs, and behind it, another soft drumming like a second heartbeat. An energy I instinctually know is his life, gently humming through me.

"I can feel you," I say, pressing my other hand to my chest.

Alaric leans in close until his mouth is only a hair's breadth away.

The small distance is too much, and I lean forward, and press my lips to his. Alaric deepens the kiss, drawing a moan from me.

After a minute, he breaks away, releasing my hand. The skin is completely healed—no cut or scar remains as proof of the oath.

"Is… is that it?" I ask, breathless from his kiss and the hum of sensations created by his proximity.

"Yes," he says, voice gravelly. "We are bound."

I start to ask how it works when Alaric's mouth crushes against mine. All questions fade away as desire sparks.

The sharp points of his fangs scrape my bottom lip

as his tongue slips inside, tangling with mine. His hands trail over my ribs and stomach, continuing their path lower and lower.

His hands grip the backs of my thighs. Alaric lifts me up, pinning me to the wall with his hips. I wrap my legs around his waist. I slide my hands up the hard planes of his chest and around his neck.

I can feel his desire for me, not just in his embrace but through the oath we made. It would be so easy to lose myself in him completely.

Alaric's hands slip over my body, bunching up the shirt that was once his. He pulls it over my head and flings it away, leaving my feverish skin pressed to the cold stone. I gasp. A low chuckle rumbles from his chest.

I claw at his shirt, surprised when it shreds as easily as cobwebs beneath my fingers. Alaric raises me higher, adjusting our position. His fingers tease, inching closer to my entrance. I writhe against him, needing to feel him in me.

A dark smile forms on his lips as he sinks two fingers into my core. I make a small, throaty noise. Then he slowly pulls his hand back, sliding out. My whimper morphs into a moan as his long fingers push deep.

Need builds with every stroke. I rock against his hand each time he pumps into me. He tilts his head, watching my every reaction, every flush, taking in every gasp and moan. His touch is exquisite, but I need….

"More," I breathe, "I need more."

He lifts me higher to shuck off his remaining clothing. Then slowly, he lowers me until the top of his cock presses against my core, holding me there as his mouth covers mine. The kiss makes me dizzy as he teases me, moving his tip back and forth over my aching center until I mewl against his lips.

Alaric breaks our kiss. Endless blue eyes drink me in, as if he's memorizing everything about this moment. He doesn't look away as he lowers me down onto him, stretching and filling me inch by inch, with agonizing slowness.

I tangle a hand into his hair, gliding the other over the scars on his chest and arms, to the corded muscles of his back. I cling to him, wanting more but utterly powerless as he takes his time.

Alaric pauses when he's only halfway inside me. He lifts my arms, one at a time, capturing my wrists and pinning them above my head.

Warm breath skates over my skin as he groans against my neck. With one powerful thrust, he seats himself fully inside, filling and stretching me with his thick girth. He pulls back and begins moving with long, gentle strokes.

We savor the sensation of our bodies moving together, and our hearts beating in tandem. It's not long before need wins out. I moan against his mouth as he thrusts again and again, faster and faster.

There will be a price for our actions tonight, but right now, I don't care. Anything—*everything*—we've been through—is worth it for this moment... worth having him inside me, being binding myself to him, owning his heart and surrendering mine to him. This man is worth it in every conceivable way.

Breaking away, I drag a series of kisses along his jaw. "I love you, Alaric," I whisper.

He nips at my neck, fangs scraping my skin, as my core clenches around him. He continues to push me toward the feeling that's coiling low in my belly. My legs tighten around his waist, trying to pull him closer.

Alaric whispers softly against my shoulder, but I don't hear what he says because I'm already falling. My orgasm crashes through me. He moves faster, driving himself harder and deeper until he's pulled toward his own climax. I feel him thicken, and with one more powerful thrust, he finds his release, and we fall into each other, wave after wave.

He lets go of my wrists, and I wrap my arms around his neck, holding tightly to him. Gradually, our fevered movements slow. Alaric rests his forehead against mine, as our chests rise and fall with matching breaths.

Slowly, he unwinds my legs, holding me in his arms, then carries me toward the bed.

I throw my head back and laugh. "I can walk."

Alaric grins wickedly. "Then I suppose I have not done my job thoroughly enough."

CHAPTER TWENTY-SIX

CLARA

There's so much to take in it's overwhelming. I'm human, but from this point on, I'll remain frozen in time, with the lifespan of a vampire. I knew it meant forever, but I never felt that word as I do now.

It's a yawning field, stretching out with no end. I can *feel* time as if it's a tangible thing. And it takes my breath away.

"Do you regret this, my dear Clara?" he breathes against my skin.

Our limbs entwined, I cling to him, nuzzling my face against his throat, soaking up his warmth, and inhaling the musky, smoky scent that is uniquely him. Even the bed isn't too small, too lumpy, or crooked. Instead, it and everything else is flawless.

He makes the world perfect.

"Never, you ridiculous vampire. I should be offended you even entertained the idea that such a thing could be possible."

He chuckles and trails kisses over my shoulder and along my collarbone to the hollow of my throat. "Say it again."

"Mmm?" I mumble unintelligently, my heavy eyelids closing as his lips travel ever more south.

Exhaustion wraps around my mind and in my muscles—but I don't want to sleep, I don't want to miss a single moment with him.

Alaric shifts, rising up, his arms creating a cage around me. Cold air brushes over my bare front. My eyes snap open to find him smiling down at me with a look on his face that I've never seen in anyone's eyes before.

Love, I realize. Pure and selfless love radiates from him. He could never speak another word for the rest of our lives, and I would never doubt for a second how he feels.

Overcome by a sudden wave of emotion, tears spring up, prickling the back of my eyes, but I push them down. It's almost too much at once, and still, I wouldn't trade any part of it for anything in the world.

My heart is full. I don't know how I can contain the sheer amount of love for this man without something giving. Saying I love you opened a floodgate, and I haven't been able to close it again or slow it.

"I love you…"

Alaric shifts to lie beside me again. I sigh, relaxing into him and wanting to soak him up. Strands of his mussed hair fall across his forehead. His long, dark lashes fan over his cheeks as his gaze comes to rest on my lips.

"I love you, Alaric Devereaux."

Those words fill me with peace. I have never thought much of love, always considering it a hindrance. My parents married out of love, and it didn't last. The lives they wanted were vastly different. They thought they could find a way around it, and their love ended up fading with their youth.

Once, I thought I loved Xander, but now it was something else—a familiarity in a small town with little to no prospects and a desire to escape. I never longed for Xander, never craved him. I was little more than a girl clinging to a future I thought I wanted, a future that would have been safe and easy, but it was never love.

With Alaric, it is entirely different. Nothing about being with him has ever been easy. With an uncertain future ahead of us, I will walk forward to whatever it brings as long as we're together.

I will do anything it takes to protect it, to protect him, and I know he would do the same. He makes my heart sing and brings color to a world that was dreary and empty before he walked into my life.

It wasn't until he sent me away without so much as a goodbye that I realized I wanted something more, something no one ever dared to want before, something different. Adventure, risk, a friend who showed me what true kindness is... It was with everything, every action, every mark, that he well and truly claimed my heart.

I will forever regret the pain I caused him by taking Rosalie's life, but I will always treasure what came after.

Alaric places a quick kiss on my lips, then a second one, slow and lingering. He pulls away far too soon for my liking. I half-growl at the distance between us, eliciting a dark, throaty laugh from him.

"Look," he whispers, motioning to the space I loathe.

Shadows dance between us. I watch the dark tendrils swirling toward me and then back to him like a beating heart.

"You're doing that," he says. "You're pulling me— my power—to you."

I lift a hand and run my fingers through the smoky wisps. Straightening my fingers, I let go. The power fades as if it were never there, then I relax back into the pillow of his arm. Surrounded by the warmth of his embrace, I let my eyes close.

Halfway to sleep, Alaric nuzzles my jaw. His lips tease my jaw with feather-light kisses.

"A single moment with you is worth more than a thousand years with anyone else," he murmurs.

My heart flutters like there's a swarm of butterflies in my chest as it did in anticipation of the first time he kissed me. Alaric runs his hands down my ribs to my hips, his fingers flexing. My eyes snap open, and I want nothing more than to feel every inch of his skin against mine.

"You will get used to it," he says with a lopsided grin. There is joy and sorrow in his expression. "Oath binding is rare. It makes us vulnerable to have that unfettered connection with another. Humans will experience things with an intensity similar to a vampire." I must have made a noise because Alaric laughs softly and kisses my temple. "There is nothing to worry about, my dear Clara. Your emotions will even out as you learn to temper them, and your strength will increase to half that of a vampire."

I will my racing heart to slow, wondering if he can feel it. This is not something we ever discussed or planned. It was a rash decision, but it was the right one, and I will never regret it for a moment.

Elizabeth might crown him consort, but now, regardless of what happens to me, she will never control him again. A dark corner of my heart revels with a spark of satisfaction and spite, bringing a curl to my lips.

"There is more, but I will have my fun as you discover it."

I shiver at the promise of finding exactly how we are bound together and how it differs from the mark.

Alaric lifts his head and glances out the window. "Dawn will be here in a few hours."

The smile falls from his handsome face, our happiness dampened by the reality brought by the ever-looming sunrise.

"What do we do now?" I ask. As much as I would love to remain in this blissful bubble, reality will come for us whether we are ready or not. "Elizabeth will figure out the truth during the coronation when she tries to oath bind you."

"We will leave tonight," he says after a long moment.

Crawling out of bed, an uncertain silence fills the air as we quickly dress for the upcoming day.

Alaric straightens his collar then runs his fingers through his hair.

I gaze at the outside world, glaring at the impending dawn. Licking my lips, I start to what he's planning, and stop when I realize it doesn't matter. But there is something that does.

"What about the others?" I ask.

"The others?"

I pick up my boots and sit on the edge of the bed. "Cassius, Della, and Lawrence. They risked their lives to help me... I'm worried Elizabeth will kill them after we leave."

Alaric kneels before me, taking my hands in his. "She won't. Before the Red Hunt, Lawrence came with news that you would be alone last night. While you were away, Elizabeth compelled me to kill you on sight, so she was more than happy to send me with him. Della is of Lawrence's line and cannot act against him."

"Elizabeth has been threatening to kill Cassius if he doesn't keep me under control. He saved my life... I can't let her—"

"If you left on your own, she would kill him to serve as an example to others. But with me, she will only blame you for breaking the compulsion. Cassius and I have always been rivals, and she knows that, he is the last vampire she would ever suspect. They will all be fine." Alaric releases my hands and stands.

"You're sure?" I bite the inside of my cheek.

"I promise. If she went after one, she would have

to go after all three. And that would only make the entire court believe they can defy her."

His reassurance eases my heart. Pulling my boots up, I stand, jutting my chin out. "What can I do to help get us ready?"

"Pack a light bag. Keep it to things that cannot be easily replaced. We can buy anything else when we stop."

There is precious little I care for. I do a mental scan of my belongings, and besides a change or two of clothes, the only things I want are the tattered book under my bed, and the night-forged dagger Alaric gave to me when we first struck our bargain.

It feels like a lifetime ago that I wanted nothing more than to kill him and live a life in a small town, scraping by. Now, I know that life would have been lonely and unfulfilling. I was never free until I left Littlemire. He may have claimed me, but in doing so, he offered me a life by his side I never dreamed possible.

"I suppose that is almost already taken care of," I say with a smile.

Alaric picks up his jacket from the floor and smacks it a few times to get the dust off and some of the wrinkles out then slides it over his ruined shirt, hiding the parts I shredded.

"Tonight," he says, straightening his cravat.

"Around noon, Cassius will come and escort you to his manor under the guise that both of you will remain there until the coronation. I will meet you shortly after the sun sets."

My heart is in my throat with anticipation. We are so close to being free of Elizabeth. I can almost taste it. It doesn't matter where we end up, but curiosity gets the better of me. "Is there a plan from there, or do you intend to make it up as we go?"

Alaric wraps me in his arms and kisses the tip of my nose. "To Progsdale—we should be able to rest there for a while before going to Valeburn in the southern mountains. We can stay there if you like or to Stormvale and sail to the Crescent Isle if you would prefer."

I look up and raise a questioning brow. "When did you have time to come up with all of this?"

"Last night, when you were snoring like a drunkard in the streets."

My jaw drops, and heat stings its way up my face. I playfully swat his shoulder. "I did no such thing!"

"Oh, but you did, my dear Clara. It's a wonder that no one in the castle came looking to see what that demon-sent noise was that nearly crumbled the foundation." He laughs and leaps back before I can swat him again. Alaric sobers quickly and continues, "We will move around a lot at first, and I will need to act human to avoid attracting undue attention to ourselves."

Alaric looks worried about that last part. He doesn't see that he is more human than most people I have ever met.

Pushing up on my toes I press a quick kiss to his mouth and run my fingers through his dark, silken strands, styling it in the way he prefers. A smile breaks out across my face. It's such a simple gesture, but it's one I can look forward to for a long time to come.

What neither of us dares to speak aloud is that we will eventually have to deal with Elizabeth. It sounds ideal—seeing the world with him, discovering all the places too small for a map.

But we can't run forever.

Once we're far enough away, we'll come up with a plan.

Alaric heaves a heavy sigh, looking over his shoulder to the door. "I must go, I can no longer put the day off."

We have an infinite amount of time ahead of us… but for now, this moment is all there is.

I nod and clasp my hands in front of me, refusing to delay him any longer.

He strides to the door, hand gripping the handle, but he doesn't open it. Alaric looks over his shoulder, taking me in for a long moment. He crosses back to me with vampire speed and cups the back of my head. His fingers tangle in my hair as he presses one final kiss to my mouth.

Reluctantly, we part so there's a breath of space between us. In the distance comes the soft chirping of an early morning winter bird.

"You have to go," I whisper.

"Tonight," he promises.

"Tonight."

CHAPTER TWENTY-SEVEN

ALARIC

I stride through the halls to my rooms. My hand pauses halfway to the doorknob when I catch the slightest trace of a scent that doesn't belong. But there is only an hour left before dawn, and I still need to change and prepare for tonight.

The neutral expression I perfected long ago slips into place as I quietly step inside. Guiding the door with my hand, it latches shut with a soft click.

Careful to keep all emotion buried, I inhale deeply, still unable to identify the scent. Below the lingering traces of humans who have come and gone over the last two weeks is something preternatural, accompanied by the metallic tang of blood—most likely vampire, but there is something off about it.

Scanning the room, I look for clues in everything

that is out of place. Though I have not been in these rooms since the night Elizabeth compelled me, a fire crackles in the hearth. If the accumulated ash below the grate is any indication, it has burned for several days.

A cup lays askew on the table, a thin layer of fresh blood pooled at the bottom. Beneath the scent of burning wood is the thick fragrance of perfume mixed with the cold night air.

It all clicks into place in a matter of a second. Then, right on cue, the doors to my sleeping chambers open, and Elizabeth sashays into the room.

She smiles warmly as if her presence here is nothing out of the ordinary. My hackles rise, apprehensive of yet another trap. I draw a discreet breath—wolf shifter blood to cover her natural cloyingly sweet scent—and my suspicions are confirmed.

Remaining silent and still, I wait for her to speak.

Large lavender eyes and painted blood red lips make her skin appear snow white. Everything about Elizabeth, from her looks to her soft voice, is designed to make her seem young, innocent, and desirable to men. It is nothing more than a façade to hide the dark, twisted creature under it.

The visage that inspires humans to fall willingly at her feet only reminds me of my time spent trapped by her powers. Elizabeth slowly stripped away my humanity with every word and action she compelled onto me. Held prisoner in my own body. I watched helplessly as she molded me into the monster she always wanted me to become.

"Good morning, my sweet prince. I trust you slept well?"

I cannot be sure if there is a bite to her words or if it's my own paranoia. It's a simple enough question, not requiring a verbal answer, so I dip my chin in a reverent nod.

Elizabeth stretches her long legs over the length of the settee. Judging from the cup with traces of blood, she has been waiting here for some time—hours before the Red Hunt was scheduled to end.

She motions to the chair across from her, indicating for me to sit. I obey her silent command without hesitation. Those eyes watch me with unnerving focus.

"You have been busy, my prince," Elizabeth says conversationally.

Still, I say nothing. She is waiting for a tell, for an error so slight that it will give away the truth.

With a quiet hum, she returns to watching. Observing. Her long slender fingers dance back and forth over the delicate chain of her necklace. The way she watches me is not unusual, but it is no less unnerving.

"Stand," she orders.

I obey.

Then tersely she orders, "Come."

I take the three steps to stand before her.

Elizabeth drops her legs off the edge of the settee in a way that intentionally drags the hem of her dress up, showing more of her thigh. Reaching out, she takes my hand in hers—the opposite of the one I used to oath bind to Clara—then rises to her feet.

She traces her finger over the bones of my hand and knuckles, then turns it over to follow the lines of my palm. "I hope you enjoyed your hunt with Lawrence last night." Elizabeth's finger stills as she looks up at me through her frosted lashes. "It seems you finally caught your prey."

"Yes, my queen," I say.

After Cassius took Clara to his estate, Elizabeth ordered me to hunt Clara down and kill her upon her return. I would have succeeded last night if her skin hadn't been coated in nightshade. Luckily, the blood seeping from her wound blinded me to the sedative's syrupy scent.

"Good," she purrs. "Because tonight I want you all to myself."

In the span of a heartbeat, she slices my palm and

then hers. Sliding her fingers through mine, Elizabeth presses our palms together, torquing my wrist at an angle that me to my knees.

My eyes widen.

She is attempting to oath bind me here and now, even though the coronation is still over a month away.

There is no exchange of power... nothing more than the two of us holding hands as our wounds heal.

I want to rip my hand from hers, but she—

"Did you *honestly* think I wouldn't notice?" she hisses through her teeth. Thin fingers tighten, pressing down, just shy of snapping my bones. "I don't know how you did it, Alaric, but you broke my compulsion."

There is no use continuing my deception. I grit my teeth and snarl as I attempt to jerk my arm free, but she holds fast. We stare each other down in silence. I wait for her to realize the full extent to which I've defied her.

Elizabeth's delicate nostrils flare. Tremors of fury rack her body as her skin turns ice cold against mine. With a scream that rattles the knocked over glass, she releases me and backs up.

"You are already oath bound..." Her chest heaves with ragged breaths. Elizabeth's face turns red, her entire body shaking with rage. Veins bulge in her neck. "You oath bound yourself to that *human?*"

She drags her nails down her arms, scratching long jagged lines into her flesh that heal almost immediately. Her fingers tangle in her perfect curls until her hair is knotted and pulled free of the careful style. Strands come loose, snarled around her fingers.

I stand, letting the cold, empty mask slide over my features, and remain silent.

"How dare you defy me? *I made you.* I gave you *everything*—this life, this unimaginable power." Her arms stretch out at her sides, fingers curling into claws as if she will rip the demons and saints from the Otherworld with her bare hands. "And this is how you repay me? By going against me at every turn… for some wretched human!"

Regardless of how benevolent she sees herself, we both know she forced me into this life. That I had refused her, wanting nothing to do with anything she offered. Even as I lay in the dirt, dying, I denied her. It was only when she fatally injured Rosalie in front of me that I conceded to Elizabeth's wishes.

As her voice dies off, her eyes blaze red with her demon's power. Her nostrils flare as she attempts to regain her composure. In the more than two hundred years I have known her, Elizabeth has always maintained complete control of her emotions.

If I wasn't witnessing it now, I would not have thought her capable of throwing a fit. It's all I can do to keep from smiling in satisfaction. This is the beginning of my revenge for all that she has stolen from me.

Elizabeth pushes back a lock of hair from her forehead before smoothing her hands over her dress. "Do not think this will go unpunished."

Placing two fingers in her mouth, she whistles.

Within seconds, the familiar beat of Kharis's feathered wings on the air approaches. Elizabeth snatches up the discarded cup on the table and holds out her arm for the demon to land.

Reaching up to her shoulder, she pulls out a long needle hidden in the seam of her dress. Elizabeth's gaze remains steadfast as she pierces the raven's neck. The demon bird doesn't flinch or protest.

Blood pours into the cup until it is nearly full—a feat that should be impossible considering the bird's size.

Elizabeth slides a finger over the wound, sealing it. Kharis turns their beady red eyes on me and caws once before flying away, passing through the door like vapor.

Holding the cup of blood out, Elizabeth jerks her chin. "Drink."

I take the cup and bring it to my nose, sniffing the

thick liquid, then lower it without drinking. Ripples dance across the surface of the blood.

"Only death can break an oath," I remind her.

"My prince, do not dare tell me what I know. I am your queen, I created you. Now, drink the blood, for your insolence."

"What punishment can I expect from this?" I demand.

"Would you rather I send for the girl and have her drink in your place?"

I growl, low in my throat, but inside, my gut twists. Elizabeth is not making an idle threat. She wants me to refuse, to give her reason to rip Clara's heart out and feel it beating in her hand.

"I have agreed to be your consort in exchange for Clara's safety. That was our deal. I never swore to be compelled or oath bind myself to you—those are demands you added without agreement or consent after the fact. I have not gone back on my end of the bargain."

"Yes, punishment for her past crimes and any she may commit in the future." A dark smile that holds no sliver of warmth creeps over her face. "But I never said she is above being *your* punishment."

Clara and I should have left the second we completed the oath. We never should have lingered. I trusted Elizabeth to keep her word when we struck our bargain. But she was deceptive and always planned to make Clara suffer because even after all this time, I still cannot love her.

"Would knowing what you'll face really help?"

"Yes."

Elizabeth presses the tip of her tongue against a fang as she considers my request. "Since you are the consort the oracle's prophesy promised, I will tell you." The corners of her mouth twitch. "It will cause you unbearable pain."

"What aren't you telling me?"

Elizabeth scoffs. "I've told you what you need to know. It is time to make your decision—the blood or the girl's life."

To refuse would mean forfeiting Clara's life here and now… if I obey and bear this punishment, then she will be safe.

"I will drink," I say. When surprise lights her eyes, I hold up a hand. "In exchange for one thing."

Her lip curls. "Is it not enough that I allow her to live?"

"I want Cherno's freedom. Release my demon and never cage, hurt, or imprison them in anyway ever again."

She laughs. "Is that all?"

"You mean other than Clara's safety if I do this? Yes." I reiterate, knowing Elizabeth will attempt to change the terms to exclude Clara if given half a chance.

"We are agreed. *Now drink.*"

The oath has connected Clara to Cherno as well.

I throw my head back, swallowing the contents in two gulps, and force the cold blood down my throat. Kharis's power settles heavily in my stomach, thick and sour. Bitterness coats my tongue—the lingering taste of rot. It slithers through my veins.

I wait for the pain she promised.

The glass slips from my hand and shatters against the floor as realization comes too late. My head snaps up, and I meet Elizabeth's cold, lavender gaze.

Cursed blood.

Her lips curls into a wicked smile. The curse will strip every last bit of who I am away, leaving me as an empty shell for her to use as she pleases.

The fate of the cursed is always death.

I summon Cherno through our connection even as it's being blocked, like walls slamming into place around it.

Find Clara. Stay with her.

Kharis's foreign power slides over me, muting my own and leaching my strength. It claws and scrapes against the oath bond... but it can only mute it, numbing me to its existence.

The world tilts. I stumble sideways. It takes

everything I have to fight against her power, but she is gaining, and in the end, she will win. I fall to my knees, clutching my throat as I glare up into her horrible face.

"You lied," I snarl.

Ringing sounds in my ears, loud and shattering. My blood feels as though it's transforming into a sluggish, icy river, numbing me to everything as it works its way through my muscles. It starts at my toes and moves upward.

Elizabeth saunters over, crouching down and bringing her serene face to eye level. She cups my cheek and leans in to whisper in my ear. "I did not lie to you, my prince. I promised you pain..." Elizabeth's eyes sparkle as she basks in her victory. "What could be more painful to you than being demon cursed and entirely under my control?"

I feel as though I'm drowning. Suffocating. Choking. Elizabeth's power coats my heart in a block of ice, then inches up, caressing my mind and stealing everything. Thoughts and memories slip through my fingers like trying to hold water in a tight fist.

Everything I have ever felt for Rosalie, for Clara, for anyone I have ever known is slowly buried in a grave, hidden until they are nothing more than distant dreams that will burn away with the light of the rising sun.

We never cared about any of them anyway, a strange voice whispers into the dark of my mind.

Straightening my spine, I blink at the flaxen-haired woman before me with lashes like ice and eyes the color of spring flowers. She takes my hands in hers, and together we rise to our feet.

I don't know who I am or how I got here.

Those things are not important.

The only thing that matters is that I am here, with her… with my queen.

My allegiance is to my queen.

That singular truth echoes where insignificant thoughts used to occupy. It is the only thing I care about, the only thing I need to know.

I feel nothing but the desire to please my queen…

And hunger.

Hunger for blood.

CHAPTER TWENTY-EIGHT

CLARA

With a final sweeping glance of the room, I nod a farewell to the drafty room that has served as a sanctuary and prison. I've packed what I need. Even if I had to leave empty handed, it wouldn't matter as long as Alaric and I were together.

I press my hand against my stomach to calm the knots that have formed over the last hour. It's barely past sunrise.

So why can't I shake the sensation that something is wrong?

A sharp pain pierces my skull, pulsing and searing. Nausea rolls through me, and I hiss against the sudden onslaught.

Light scratching against the door draws my

attention past my discomfort. It's too soon for it to be Cassius. If it were, he would have barged in when I didn't immediately answer.

Turning around, I open the door. No one is there. Slowly, I stick my head out and look from left to right. The hall is deathly silent.

"Clara." The small voice drags my gaze down to Cherno, crumpled at the threshold of my room. Large, dark eyes blink up at me. The red glow of their power has dimmed to a warm brown and their wings are splayed out, limp.

My heart lurches into my throat. I crouch and scoop the tiny demon into my hands, then hastily close the door. Leaning against the wood, I slide to the ground, cradling Cherno to my chest.

"What happened to you?" I whisper. "Where have you been?"

Their small front claws wrap around my thumb as I lift them to my face. Pale lines are branded into their wings, some new, some partially faded.

Cherno doesn't speak for a long time. "The queen," they say eventually. "She locked me in a cage of night-forged silver… and now she has Alaric."

I swallow thickly. I know the answer before I even ask, but still hope. "He's in the cage now?"

Cherno shakes their head.

Elizabeth can lock him up, but she can't compel him

ever again. Closing my eyes, I take a calming breath, then look at the tiny creature in my hands.

"He is demon cursed," they say in a small, broken voice.

"That's impossible. You've been his demon for—"

They shake their head. "It's different with *her*. She can curse vampires and humans with Kharis's power." Cherno's body shudders, whether in fear, weakness, or sorrow, I can't tell. Possibly all three. "The queen has destroyed his mind—he is nothing more than a shell. Alaric is gone."

"She knows, Clara." Cherno's voice breaks through the sound of my world being rent into a million pieces. "Elizabeth waited in his quarters for him to return. She realized he was already bound to you when she attempted to oath bind him."

I squeeze my eyes shut. That quiet second heartbeat is gone, and I can no longer sense his presence. Grasping desperately for the bond that connects us, my pulse quickens.

It's there. Unbroken by the curse. Except...

Something slimy separates us, muting what I know is there—bright, blinding, and utterly brilliant. The barrier is like looking into a dark room through old, thick glass, warped by time and gravity, clouded and scratched by years of weather and grit.

I love you, I whisper down the ghostly connection as if he can somehow get my message.

There is no reply, only deafening silence.

Everything I did, has been for nothing. Exactly as the oracle had warned. Ophelia told me the spell wouldn't save him, but I ignored her, and once again, Elizabeth found a way to trap him.

I swallow the bile rising in my throat.

This can't be it. There must be something I can do. Even if all my effort and sacrifice only ever amounts to nothing, I can't give up—*I refuse to give up*—until he's free from her for good. Elizabeth will have to kill me first.

With shaking hands, I place Cherno on my shoulder and struggle to stand. I nearly trip over my own feet as I rush to set the demon on the pillow. "You can stay with me for as long as you want," I say. "There is something I need to do, but I'll be back soon."

By the time I close the door behind me, I'm struggling to catch my breath. My heart is beating too hard. I want to scream and rage and tear the world to pieces until Elizabeth lets him go.

He was free.

She might as well have killed him.

No. No, no, no, no...

I thrust my fingers into my hair, shoving it off my

face. Then I lose the battle against the heartache. One hot tear spills over, tracking down my cheek, then another and another.

Have I risked my life again and again only to have Alaric back for a few hours? Is that all the time fate has deigned to allow us?

Wiping roughly at the tears with my sleeve, I make my way downstairs and through the back halls. Servants give me strange looks as I shoulder past.

I take the winding spiral stairs down, running past the training room where Cassius spent countless hours teaching me how to defend myself. My ragged breaths and pulse fight to drown the other out.

As soon as I reach the landing, I snatch up the first torch I pass and race to the end of the hall. The light chases the shadows from the hidden stairway as I descend into the lower levels.

Varin helped me once, they can do it again.

Bargaining with a demon is reckless. Insane. They can't be trusted. But it doesn't matter. This is the only option left.

Whatever the demon wants is worth it—*Alaric is worth it.*

At the bottom of the stairs, I let the torch fall from my hand. It clatters against the stone, still rocking when I shove through the door. I sprint down the narrow hall, my sights set on the lone occupied cell.

Sweat clings to the edges of my hairline, more noticeable in the chilly air of the lower level. The familiar stench of mold and rot clings to my skin like damp clothes.

I slip quietly into the cell. A sigh slithers through the dark, radiating from all directions. Calm and cool.

The demon shifts, and their glowing eyes settle on me. Pale light flickers through the bars near the top of the door, highlighting the edges of Varin's dark, misshapen form.

"I am sorry," they say quietly.

Fresh tears sting my eyes, but I force them back. There is no time for that.

"Tell me how to save him."

The demon hunches lower, shaking their head regretfully. "There is a reason they call it a curse."

My fingers curl into my palms, nails digging into the soft skin. "There has to be. What do I need to sacrifice? What must I bargain away?"

"You would not—"

I stalk forward and loom over the crouching demon. "I will do whatever it takes—damn my soul to the Otherworld if I must. Tell me and I will make it happen."

From one breath to the next, Varin is curled, crouching on the ground—then they rise, knocking me to my back.

Long fingers with too many joints smack down on either side of my head, clacking their taloned points against the stone. Arms that bend and twist at sharp, painful angles hold the bony body above me. Varin slowly lowers their face to mine.

"Finally, you have come to me as you were meant to," they say. When they speak, the charred looking skin wrinkles and cracks around their mouth, exposing double rows of razor-sharp teeth that jut out at multiple angles.

Blood roars in my ears. I stare up into coal red eyes flecked with molten amber. "You've hounded me for weeks to bargain with you and asked for my trust. And now when I'm—" My suddenly dry throat strangles my words. "The compulsion, the oracle, and cursing Alaric—*you planned everything?*"

"Do not misunderstand," they hiss. "I sensed you from the moment you stepped foot inside this cursed place." Varin slides back on their haunches, pinning my legs to the ground.

I sit up, supporting my weight with my hands splayed out behind me.

"For over three hundred years, you are the first to learn of my existence. Do you think you stumbled upon, not one, but two passages to my cell by chance?"

My blood boils. I want to wriggle out from under

them and leave. But I can't. "You manipulated me," I spit out.

"You are a rarity among humans, strong enough to withstand my powers… And I need you, Clara."

I want to reach for the night-forged dagger but refrain, knowing full well that I can't use it. Because no matter what they've done, Varin is the only hope I have left. "Tell me honestly, are you responsible for Elizabeth cursing Alaric so I would have no choice but to bargain with you?" I demand.

The demon lists their head at an odd angle. "I have never lied to you."

"Answer me."

"Do not give me so much credit. I cannot control the choices others make," Varin says quietly, and I find myself leaning in to catch every word. "I have guided your path, but I could not foresee the queen cursing the man she wants at her side, knowing it will eventually kill him."

They shift their weight off me, freeing my limbs. I scramble back out of their reach but remain seated. I don't trust my legs to hold me up.

Varin stretches their arm out and slowly unfurls their fingers to reveal the slender, silver band. "But yes, it was always my plan to bind you to me with this."

I suck in a breath and hold it.

"Agree to this bargain, Clara Valmont, because I need your help. And now… you need mine."

My eyes lock onto the ring, unable to turn away. In a castle full of immortals, I am far from the strongest being here. Questioning the offered help I desperately need is foolish, but I need to understand. "I'm human. What could I possibly do for a demon? If you bargained with Elizabeth—"

Their snarl breaks the ring's hold on me. I snap my head up and meet eyes glowing with power.

"It is because of her that I am locked in this cell… and that is why I help you. Bargain with me, help free me from her, and in return, I will help you save your oath bonded."

Intending to accept, my lips part. But then I hesitate. Agreeing to anything the demon wants is one thing, but I have to ask. "How do I know you won't kill me before you fulfill your part?"

"I have watched over for you longer than you know." The demon inches closer, their chains rattle softly with the movement. "The night Elizabeth poisoned you, she believed the blood belonged to her Kharis."

"But it didn't?" I rasp.

"I replaced it with my own." The mouth on Varin's skeletal face curls into an unsettling grin.

"Why?"

"Kharis's blood would have killed you. With mine, I have the ability to heal you before you could walk into the Otherworld. Because you lived, you are stronger and will be able to wield my power and oppose hers."

I blink. Things I've forgotten begin to resurface. A conversation in the dark, Varin's hand around my throat, and the feeling of their power rushing through my veins, healing me. I nearly died that night... I *would* have died without them.

"Demons' powers can't oppose each other," I say, remembering what Cassius told me. "How will yours help me against Elizabeth?"

"That is true..." Varin taps the tips of their taloned fingers together with disquieting glee. "Of other demons, even Kharis, but not so for me. I am not the same as the demons you have known."

I shake my head. "Then... Cassius could have healed me?"

Questions burn the back of my tongue demanding to be asked—questions that most likely come with lengthy answers—but there will be time for that later.

Varin shrugs. "You lived, and that is all that matters." They press their hands to the ground lowering to bring their gaze level with mine. "Of all the options you have for comfort, why did you come to *me* in tears tonight?"

Della, Cassius, and even Lawrence would be there for me in a heartbeat if they knew. But I didn't come for that.

I set my jaw. What I need is a way to save Alaric.

"I'm not here seeking comfort," I say. "Help me, and I will free you."

Varin stretches their arm out farther. I grab for it, only for them to close their fist. "Will you not ask what freedoms you will forfeit once you willingly bind yourself to me?"

"There is no point. We both know I will concede to whatever you ask," I grind out. "Give me the ring."

"Then we are agreed."

Varin manipulated me since I arrived at Nightwich. Guiding me, whispering in the dark… saving my life, sending me to the oracle. Every kindness was self-serving, but I can't fault them for it. I would do the same to regain my freedom.

Squaring my shoulders, I say, "Yes, we are agreed."

Their long fingers unfurl. The band is bright and flawless against their charred, bone-like skin. My hand is surprisingly steady when I reach out for the ring. The metal is cool, warming slightly with my touch.

I slide it onto my left middle finger. It glows as if made from moonlight as it changes size to fit. Then it dims, appearing to be nothing more than an unadorned band. I turn it with my thumb—snug but not too tight.

Varin's chains don't fall away, nor do they transform into an animal… And I remain as human as ever. Even the metal band feels like nothing more than cold steel.

"We are connected only through the ring until you are strong enough to bear all of my power," Varin says. The curved edge of their long, taloned fingers run gently down my face. "Irrevocably binding myself to you now would only bring you a cursed death."

My gut tells me that there is more left unsaid. But I meant it when I vowed to sacrifice whatever is necessary. Even if it costs me every last scrap of my humanity, I will give this demon whatever they demand.

"Now," I say, turning my hand and watching the way the dim light glints off the metal. "Tell me how to break the curse."

"*Not so fast, my little human,*" Varin's speaks inside my mind as clearly as if they had spoken out loud.

"*There is more to donning a band and having unfettered power at your fingertips. You must first learn to bear the weight of it before you can wield it.*"

Vampires call me slayer, but I refuse to take up their meaningless mantle.

Instead, I will become something entirely different.

Something powerful that has yet to be named.

I lift my chin and meet the demon's eyes. Gold embers flicker like fire against the intense, crimson power.

"When do we start?"

Continue the story in
THE VAMPIRE CROWN

Or visit **www.thevampiredebt.com** for more information about the series as well as maps, custom art, playlists, bonuses, giveaways, and more!

THANK YOU

Thank you for reading The Vampire Oath. It's always so much fun to explore new worlds and old, and to watch my characters come to life on the page.

If you enjoyed reading The Vampire Oath, then please consider leaving an honest review on Amazon, Bookbub, or Goodreads.

Reviews are so, so important for helping other readers decide whether or not to read a certain book. They don't need to be long or super descriptive. A single sentence or a few words is all that's needed. Positive, neutral, or negative feelings are all valid. All I ask is that you be mindful not to spoil the story or the ending for your fellow readers.

Stay in touch and be among the first to learn about new releases, cover reveals, character art, special offers, exclusive content (first few chapters, bonus scenes, and spontaneous shorts), and more by signing up for my newsletter!

www.aliwinters.com/newsletter

ADULT TITLES

SHADOW WORLD GOTHIC EPIC ROMANTASY:

The Vampire Debt series:

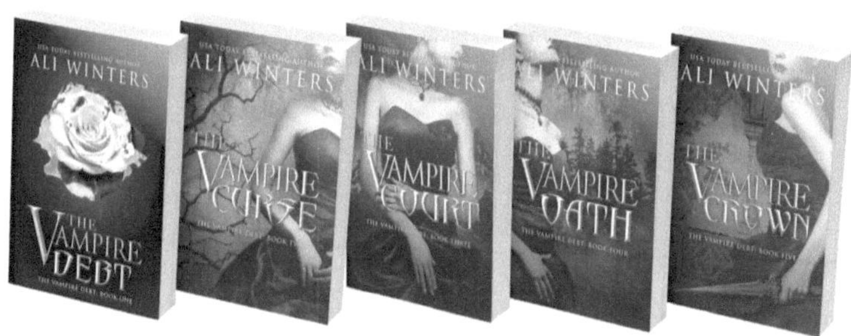

It is a truth universally acknowledged that a single

Vampire in possession of a good fortune must be in want of a mortal snack.

Learn more: **www.thevampiredebt.com**

SHADOW WORLD: STAND ALONES:

WICKED PRINCE OF FROST: an epic gothic romantasy

He promised to heal her broken heart, but if she's not careful, he may just end up taking it for himself.

Learn more: **www.aliwinters.com/shadowworld**

THE VAMPIRE TRAP: A Shadow World novella

When a series of murders breaks out across the city of Sangate, all evidence points to the most powerful vampire in the city.

Learn more: **www.aliwinters.com/shadowworld**

STAND ALONES:

HIGH STAKES: A stand alone Urban Romantasy novella

Elle Darling takes a bounty on an item retrieval job that sounds simple enough, but soon becomes deadly when the secret surrounding it is one many would kill to possess. She could end up losing her job or worse… her life.

Learn more: **www.aliwinters.com/standalones**

YOUNG ADULT TITLES

THE HUNTED SERIES:

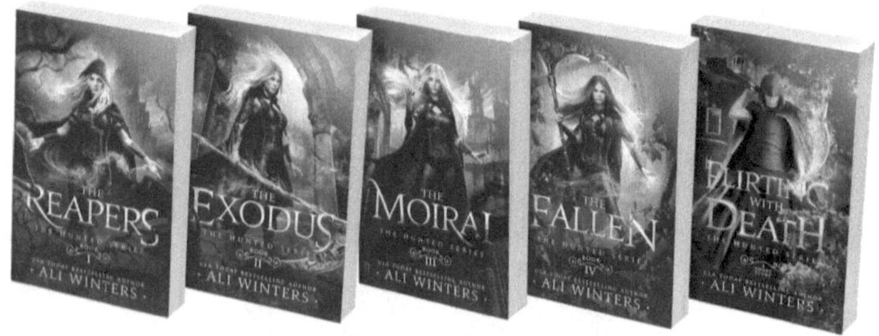

A Reaper and her mortal enemy must team up to save the balance of life and death before all is lost. Unfortunately, to succeed, one of them must die.

Learn more: **www.aliwinters.com/the-hunted-series**

IN THE END DUOLOGY:

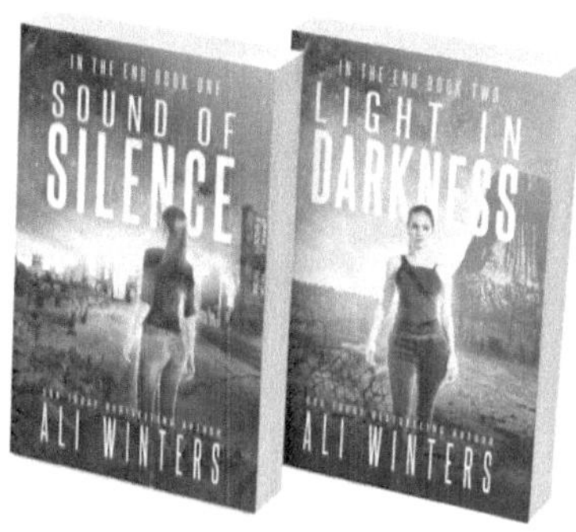

We thought we were alone in the universe. Turns out we were wrong. Dead wrong. —This book is a Romeo and Juliet retelling and contains insta-love, aliens, a virus, and zombies.

Learn more: **www.aliwinters.com/sos**

FAVOR OF THE GODS: a short story

"Like Icarus, you flew too close to the sun. Someone had to bring you back down to reality. You don't belong with princesses, heroes, or demigods."

Learn more: **www.aliwinters.com/standalones**

CAST IN MOONLIGHT

Welcome to Havenwood Falls, a small town where nobody is what you think, where truths pose as lies, and where myths blend with reality.

Cast in Moonlight is a stand alone novella in the shared world of Havenwood Falls, a multi-author collaboration.

Learn more: **www.aliwinters.com/standalones**

ABOUT THE AUTHOR

Ali Winters is the USA TODAY Bestselling author of several series filled with romance, magic, and adventure. She enjoys breaking down characters to build them up so they find their true strengths.

Her first love will always be fantasy, but she fully admits to being obsessed with coffee and T-Rex, and has a weakness for love interests that walk the line between gray and villainy.

Connect with Ali online
www.aliwinters.com

facebook.com/authoraliwinters

instagram.com/authoraliwinters

bookbub.com/authors/ali-winters

tiktok.com/@authoraliwinters